Published by City of IF, www.cityofif.com.

ISBN 0-9765477-0-8

Cover illustration by Patrick McEvoy
Interior illustrations by Leigh Dragoon
Book design by Lee Moyer

THE ARCHER'S FLIGHT

Mark Keavney

To "Araex", one of the true "City Elders". :)
Hope you like this

Mark

www.cityofif.com

For Mïa

—— Introduction ——
THE CITY OF IF

This book was created in an unusual way. It was serialized, appearing in seventeen chapters over a year's time, but that's not what's unusual about it. It was published on the Web, but that's not the unusual part either. What is unusual (and as far as I know, unique) is that this story's readers chose the actions of its main character. Each published chapter ended in some dilemma for the protagonist, Deica; the audience collectively decided what she would do (via posting and voting on a web site), and their decision led to the next chapter. This was not a group of writers offering advice on what would make the best story; rather, the readers took on Deica's role, as they would in improvisational theater or a roleplaying-type game. They decided what they would do if they were her.

Those who took part in this unusual experiment experienced something between reading a story and playing a game. They looked forward to and (I hope) enjoyed each chapter as they would a favorite novel; and they considered each decision as they might the moves of a chess game. For me as the author the process was both demanding and exhilarating: writing each chapter without knowing the next, adding new characters and places at each turn, trying to keep the story on track while the main character kept slipping off in unexpected directions—I would have pulled my hair out if I hadn't been having so much fun.

You hold in your hands the product of that experience. The story has been edited, but the basic plot of this book is the same as that of the story told on the Web. And it bears its birthmarks: it's a story filled with twists and surprises, a story of choices. It's not a story that any one person would ever think up, and I hope that it will open the door to many other stories that no one person would ever think up.

This is already starting to happen. Other storygames, set in the Wheel and in other worlds, are going on right now on the City of IF web site, www.cityofif.com. To me, this is the beginning of a new art form that combines the creativity of linear storytelling with the interactivity of games. If you want to see this first-hand, stop by and visit. The City of IF is a wide and wonderful place, and friendly strangers are always welcome.

Mark Keavney
March 21st, 2005

—— Prologue ——
THE MATING

To reach him she crossed half the Wheel—walking, slithering on her belly as a snake, taking to wing in dragon-form when she dared. Her people called her mad, for to be seen in his city bore the penalty of death, and to mate with him risked far worse. But her need was as deep as the ocean. She didn't look back.

He was old and strong as only the immortal can be. Long ago he'd been a god. Now he was a king, sitting on a white throne and ruling over a foreign people. Pride drove him to take what she offered, pride that scoffed at the ancient laws and saw her defiance as a challenge. He let her come.

They met in his Great Hall, but the need for secrecy drew them lower, down to the caverns underneath. There among the slippery rocks and the water dripping from the walls, they came together. Their huge bodies smashed the stone, fiery breaths turning the water to steam, roars echoing through the empty caves. Far above, the ground shook and the people trembled. Two thousand times the Wheel had turned since their kind had last coupled.

When it was done and she had what she needed, he collapsed on the cave floor, spent. But she rose, lightened, and climbed out to the open air. Laughing, she launched herself into the night sky, burning with joy, breathing great plumes of fire, announcing to the Wheel what she had done.

And the people who saw her were filled with fear, for they knew that their world would never be the same again.

—— CHAPTER ONE ——
THE FREAK

Year 4

Once upon a time there was a little girl with ten fingers and ten toes. One two three four five six seven eight nine ten makes ten and that's your name says Gramma. My name isn't really ten it's Deica but Deica means ten Grampa says. Grampa is big and hairy. Gramma kisses me and smells like honey. She made honey-cakes for Grampa and gave me some.

> *shake shake shake*
> *down comes the stake*
> *shake shake shake*
> *out goes the snake*

I sang that song when I played with Gesel. Mama says Gesel should do her work and stop playing with me. Gesel's a slave so she has to do what Mama says. I'm not a slave but I have to do what Mama says too.

Gramma's got ten fingers too. But Grampa and Gramma and Mama don't have ten toes like me because they're centaurs. I'm not a centaur. Gesel's got toes because she's a sheephead. I'm not a sheephead either.

—*What am I?*

—You're a lazy brat who's going to get her rear spanked, says Mama.

—You're a two-legged freak, says Anisa. You're not like anybody.

Anisa is my big sister. She's going to get married when she grows up. I'm not going to get married because Mama says no one would want me.

—*When I grow up I'm going to ride a big horse all over the Wheel.*

—Mama laughs: Yeah, when cows talk. Anisa laughs too: Yeah, when unicorns fly.

—*What am I?*

Gramma's sad.

—You're just Deica, that's all.

Year 9

It's Reconciliation Day, so everyone is supposed to be nice to each other. Mama even gave Gesel some sweetbread and the rest of the night off after she finishes cleaning up. We all eat together in the big room—Grampa, Acrios, Cousin Hiram, Gramma, Mama, Anisa, and me. I have to stand up. Mama lets me sit down when we eat in the kitchen because I only have two legs, but I have to stand up at the table in the big room so that I'll look almost like a normal centaur girl.

Grampa and Acrios went hunting yesterday and shot a deer. Now Grampa cuts it up and prays to Aeneas the Sacrificer and Agnus the Sacrifice and all the Makers on Earth to keep us safe from Serpents, and we all get some. I don't eat much because I'm so small, but the meat is warm and tastes good and doesn't give me a stomachache the way dried grass does.

Acrios is my brother. He goes to school and learns history and writing and archery. He talks a lot. He says that he's the teacher's scribe in history and he beat Perineus at a game of Aeneas' March and he shot a bulls-eye from fifty paces. Grampa says that we may not have the greatest school on the Wheel, but as long as he's alive Acrios will always get the finest archery lessons. I say that I want to learn archery too but no one hears me.

Cousin Hiram is from Leucta. He's fat and he wheezes. He eats a lot of meat and talks with his mouth full. He asks Grandpa if he could spare some white grapes to make wine with. "You must have money to burn if you're still feeding that freak," he says. Anisa sniggers and pokes me. I flush.

Later I go outside. When I was little I used to go past the stone wall into Delos, the village, but then one day when I was fetching water some of the centaur boys came to see Denophos's little freak granddaughter. They laughed at my two legs and took turns pushing me over. I tried to stand up but they were bigger than me and they pushed me into the stream and got me all muddy and wet. Gesel came and tried to help me but they were bigger than her too and they pushed her down. Then they got tired and let us go, but when Grampa heard about it he was mad and said I couldn't go off our property anymore. Gesel says the boys wouldn't have dared do that when Papa was alive.

So now I can't go past the stone wall. But I know what's out there. Outward there's the forest, which is the Wild Lands. Inward there's the village, Delos, with roads and houses and a temple and a market. Gesel says further on there are big cities with stone roads, and eleven other kingdoms besides the kingdom of centaurs and far far away a huge city at the center of the Wheel where the Emperor rules them all. I want to go there someday.

I like it outside at night. Whenever I want I can look up and see the Earth and the stars. The Earth is where the Makers live and the stars are the special Makers who protect us from monsters. As long as they're watching over you, you don't have to be afraid of anything.

I hear a sound now, far away and very beautiful, like a song. I can't understand the words. Is it calling my name? I go to the edge of the property.

—*Who's there?*

No one answers. Mama calls harshly from the house: "Deica!" She yells again: "Deica!" She doesn't see me.

I still hear the sound—a wordless, almost silent singing. It's coming from the forest where the evil things live, but it's more beautiful than anything I've ever heard. My heart flutters. I look up at the stars, take a deep breath, and scramble over the stone wall, running into the forest.

Now I'm in Wild country, the land of witches and dragons. The trees are different here, hunched and twisted, with thick branches that crowd out the Earthlight. I stumble and fall onto a bed of roots. A black lizard glares at me, then scampers up a tree.

I'm still following the sound, running, stumbling into the woods. I see dark figures ahead, singing and dancing around a fire. I can't understand what they're saying.

I creep up quietly, but one of them turns around, as if she can smell me behind her. She peers into the dark, her eyes sweeping over my hiding place, and a thrill of terror goes through me...

I come back hours later, covered with cuts and bruises from running through the thorn bushes, and my crying wakes the house. Mama beats me all night but I don't tell her what happened.

Year 13

Grandma didn't say much in the end. She slept a lot, and when she woke she'd hold Deica's hand, but her own hands were oily with black blisters on them and her throat was so swollen she could hardly speak. Then one night Deica went to sleep next to her and when she woke up Grandma was dead.

Deica cried then, just like she'd cried when she first found out, when the priest came after she'd fainted in the kitchen. He said, "It's Ekro," and Deica knew that meant Blackfever and she'd heard of lots of people who'd had Blackfever and they were all dead. Mama and Acrios and even Grandpa looked scared but Deica just cried. The priest said prayers for her and made her some special tea with herbs and Grandpa sacrificed a hen but Deica knew it wasn't going to do any good.

It only took a few days, and Deica spent it with her in her room. They didn't visit her much because they were afraid of catching it. Gesel brought the tea and Grandpa came twice but Mama only came to the door and Anisa didn't come at all. Acrios visited once, which surprised Deica. It was pretty late in the sickness and Grandma wasn't awake, and he stood with two legs in the room and two legs out and stared at her face all covered with boils.

When she could still talk she told Deica about when Deica was born. Deica always knew there was something, from the way Mama used to look away whenever they heard about babies left to die in the Wild. "We were going to leave you there too," Grandma said. Papa was at the war and Grandpa didn't think we could afford another girl, especially not a deformed one. Grandma had wanted to keep her but Mama and Grandpa were against it, so they sent out a slave with Deica in a clay pot to leave in the forest. He didn't come back after a long time so Grandpa went to look for him. Grandpa came back with the clay pot and Deica inside, crying to wake the Makers. The slave was dead; it looked like he'd been attacked by a Serpent in the forest. He must have fought the Serpent off but bled to death, so she was left there all alone. Grandpa said that if the Makers kept her safe from a Serpent attack that it was an omen they should keep her.

"So that was how you came into our home," Grandma said. "Your mama named you Deica because you were her tenth, even though there's only Acrios and Anisa and you left now."

The smoke rose from the pyre when they burned her body. It went up and up until Deica couldn't see it anymore. *When you die if you're good you go live with the Makers on Earth.* Did the smoke take Grandma to Earth then? Or did she go when she died and her body was just empty? Makers don't have bodies; they're just spirits, like the air. And they're always good to each other. *She was good to me.* Deica cried.

She cried again later that day, when she was chopping olives for the salad. Her body shook and Gesel came to hold her. But then Gesel looked at her funny and walked away. She cried some more and kept chopping. Then Mama and Gesel came and stood at the door and stared at her. She felt hot and angry. "What?" she snapped. But they just kept staring. Deica looked down and saw her hands all sweaty, with a small black blister on her knuckle. Then there was a roar in her head and everything turned black.

When she woke up she heard wailing. She was in her room and Mama was in the atrium, but Mama was crying so loud the whole house could hear her. "My baby! My baby!" She wouldn't stop. Gesel came in with a tray of water and figs that she put on Deica's side-table. She closed the door and sat down.

"Acrios has it too," Gesel said. Deica groaned. *Maybe we'll all die,* she thought. *Maybe we'll all go to the Makers together.* Gesel put her hand on Deica's forehead. Her touch felt good, cool against her skin. Gesel's hands were thick and hairy, the hands of a sheephead. *Do sheepheads get Blackfever? She should be more careful,* Deica thought as she drifted off to sleep.

The priest was in her room. He pulled back the blankets to look at her legs. It was cold. She tried to pull them up again. He opened her eyes wide with his hands, and then measured the size of the boils on her arms. Then he left. She heard voices:

"He's a strong boy, and he'll get the best care and blessings. He has excellent chances..."

"...not likely to make it. Younger and female, plus the deformity has robbed her of a strong constitution..."

"...a blessing. Cost us a good slave the day she was born and been nothing but trouble since..."

Sleep. Pain in her head. Everything was hot and far away. The blanket was heavy like iron. Gesel gave her water. The room was spinning.

—*O Gramma why did you leave me?*

—I love you, my little Deica.

—*O Gramma where are you?*

The priest was in the house. Prayers and a sacrifice. Someone painted a blessing on the door. Everything was hot, she was burning up. There was a tightness in her chest. Her skin felt strange. *I'm turning into a Serpent. My arms are shrinking and my body is black and scaly.* Then Gesel opened the door and it was all right.

More water and soup. Shrieking and crying. Her head hurt. Her blankets were sweaty. Sleep.

She was hungry. Her head still ached and she was weak but things were clearer. Gesel brought water and Deica thanked her. Her voice sounded like croaking. She went back to sleep.

The house was quiet. Deica felt tired but better. She pushed herself up. She could walk if she leaned against the wall. The house was empty. She went to the back door and looked outside. She saw them walking back from the other side of the farm, where the graves were. There was Grandpa, Mama, Anisa, Gesel, and the two farmhands, Olphos and Agenos. No Acrios. They must have just burned his body.

It took a few days before Deica felt normal again. She still had scars on her arms and legs from where the boils had burst. Anisa looked at her like she was a ghost and didn't talk to her. Mama spent all her time crying over Acrios. Deica knew she should feel bad that he was dead, but she didn't feel anything. Grandpa practiced archery in the field behind the house, all morning, every day.

There was no one to make her do chores anymore, so Deica decided to watch Grandpa practice. She walked down the path to where he used to teach Acrios. She could see the wooden target that he'd nailed to an old oak, surrounded by bales of hay to catch the arrows. Acrios's smaller bow and arrows were still in a box to the side.

The morning sun shone on Grandpa's back and hindquarters. His torso was strong and thick and his horse legs muscular, despite his long gray hair and beard. After each shot he winced and flexed his fingers. He didn't see Deica behind him.

A strange feeling possessed her. Hardly knowing what she was doing, she picked up Acrios's bow. With her heart pounding, she fitted an arrow to the string, drew it back, and let it fly.

The bow felt so magical in her hands, the motion so smooth and quick, she was sure she would hit the bulls-eye. But the arrow flew short, and stuck in the oak-roots. Deica froze, her hands still gripping the bow, sure that Grandpa would beat her.

But he only stared at her, and looked at the oak, and then back at her, for a full six or seven breaths. And then he lowered his big gray eyebrows and said, "What are you doing, girl?"

And then another miracle happened. Because though her hands shook and her mouth was dry, somehow the Makers gave her courage and a voice strong enough to say, "I want to learn."

And the faraway call of birds was the only sound in the quiet that grew in those words, touching Grandpa and her.

Year 17

Thunk! A bulls-eye. Deica smiled. Nowadays, this distance was more of a warm-up than a challenge, but it always felt good to bulls-eye.

"Now do it without your arms shaking," growled Grandpa, unimpressed as usual with her accuracy. For Grandpa, archery was more than hitting the target.

Deica nocked another arrow and pulled back, careful to keep her stance solid, her breathing even, her muscles working smoothly together. The rhythm rose up—ready, draw, release—and the arrow flew with perfect form. *Thunk!* Another bull's-eye.

Grandpa grunted. Deica suppressed another smile. For him, that was high praise.

He'd never told her why he agreed to teach her, that mad day four years ago. Maybe he was half-mad himself with the death of Acrios, or maybe he thought it was an omen from the Makers that she would dare to pick up the bow. But whatever the reason, she was grateful.

He'd been a hard teacher, and her lessons had been filled with pain. "Bend your knees!" he'd yell, as her legs spasmed from crouching too long. "Hold it! Hold it!" he'd call, as she kept the bow drawn till her arms felt like they'd fall off. But she found a way through the pain, and often ended the practices stronger than she started.

More than the physical pain, it was the rhythm of archery that had been hardest. Ready, draw, release: it sounded so simple. But for years she had jerked the draw, or held it too long, or stopped between each step. Only recently had her shots started to look like Grandpa's: one fluid motion from the time she touched the arrow until it flew into the target. Only now did she understand what he meant when he said that the release was like "snow falling from a leaf," happening when it was ready.

She nocked another arrow.

"That's enough for today," said Grandpa abruptly.

Deica looked at him in surprise. "But we've been out here less than an hour."

Grandpa motioned for her to sit down on the log bench. "Girl, it's time we talked about your future. This..." he gestured to the archery field, "For you, this leads nowhere."

He might as well have slapped her in the face. "Why did you teach me then?"

Grandpa sighed. "You have the heart of an archer, Deica. When you shoot, I see your father. But you've got the body of..." He didn't have to say it. *A freak.* A freak and a girl.

"I won't be around forever," said Grandpa. "What do you think will happen to you when I'm gone?"

"I guess that's up to Cousin Hiram," Deica said. For many reasons, she didn't like to think of Grandpa dying. When he was gone, the house and farm would belong to his cousin, who referred to her as "that freak" or "that thing."

"That's right. And that's why I want to see you settled before I go on to the Makers. You're seventeen now, past marrying age even if that were possible. There's only one path."

Deica knew what he was going to say. He'd hinted at it before.

"I spoke to the Goatfoot Priest last week. He's looking for acolytes, and he's willing to take you on despite your deformity."

The priesthood. From Grandpa's point of view, it made sense. And maybe it wouldn't be so bad. The village priest was a lecherous old satyr who was always leering at her, but as a priestess she'd be a consecrated virgin so he couldn't bother her too much. And the ceremonies and sacrifices wouldn't be hard. Sometimes when she made them at home she did feel the presence of the Makers.

But she'd be stuck in the same village for the rest of her life. And of course they'd never let her shoot again. The priesthood was like a grey cloud, dull and oppressive. For years she'd been trying to escape from it, but all she'd ever come up with were vague, crazy ideas.

"Grandpa? Isn't there something I could do in the city?"

He raised his eyebrows. "In Kerigos? What would you do there?"

"I don't know. I just thought maybe, if I could shoot, maybe someone would pay me for that."

"If you were a normal centaur boy, they might. But you..." he shrugged helplessly.

"What if I lived on my own? I could hunt for food."

"Where? You mean in the Wild Lands?"

A shiver of fear ran down her spine, remembering the time—"No, no, I just meant, maybe somewhere, somewhere else—"

Suddenly, over Grandpa's shoulder, she saw a plume of black smoke rising from the woods behind their fields. "Grandpa? What's that?"

He turned and peered into the distance. It was a few miles off, in the direction of Leucta, a neighboring village. Were they sending a signal?

"Get inside," he said in a low voice. Then, faster than she would have thought possible for a centaur his age, he turned and galloped away, leaping the stone wall that marked their property, heading for the center of Delos. Deica stared at the smoke spiraling upward, wondering what was burning.

No one could remember when the wild things had been so bold. This has always been frontier country—a watch was posted at night for stray Serpents, and the villagers all knew not to wander into the forest alone. But to have Leucta burnt to a smoking ruin in broad daylight—that was beyond anyone's nightmares.

An Elder Worm, one of the oldest and greatest terrors of the Wild Lands, had attacked Leucta. It had come from the forest with no warning, first ravaging the farms on the outskirts, then setting the main village aflame and burning the villagers to death in their own homes. None had tried to stand against it; the few who'd escaped could hardly even say what it looked like, speaking in terrified whispers only of fire, rage, and blood.

The people of Delos feared for their lives. Over the next few days, many fled Inward for the safety of the cities. The rest armed for battle and petitioned the King's Governor for aid. The Governor granted their request, sending a hero named Argus with forty veteran soldiers to kill the Worm.

Deica's family stayed. Cousin Hiram and his wife lived in Leucta, but they had been visiting Delos at the time of the attack, so now they became permanent guests of Deica's family. Grandpa dug out his old leather coat and bronze helmet from the storage shed and spent his days plotting war with Argus and the other soldiers. Mama stayed in her room sobbing in fear, leaving Deica to do the housework and serving for five people, including one who detested the sight of her.

But she hardly noticed Hiram's slights and insults now. Something much bigger was stalking her.

Even before she'd known what had happened, when Grandpa left her alone staring at the smoke from Leucta's ruin, she'd felt it, like a cold hand on her heart: fear. When she saw the survivors stagger in, dazed and ash-covered, carrying their burnt dead, it swept over her like a wave. It was an old fear, dating back to when she was nine years old, a fear that she had never spoken of, and it had grown in the silence. Now it followed her from morning to night, and hunted her in her dreams. Just getting through the day without screaming took all of Deica's strength.

And Grandpa—the only one who could have saved her—in the end he broke her heart. He was so proud to be a soldier again, so puffed up practicing with his bow and old sword ("That's genuine Bullroar workmanship," he'd brag), that he was deaf to her pleas to flee. But Deica knew that he could never stand against what was in the Wild Lands. He seemed old and frail to her now, and that made her feel more alone than ever.

Late one night, she made one last attempt to convince him to leave. She waited until he came back from meeting with the other centaurs, and she threw herself at his hooves. "Please, Grandpa, let's run away like the others. Don't go after the Worm."

He reached down and gently pulled her up. "I know you're afraid," he said. "But don't worry. Argus and his soldiers—they're amazing, like the centaurs of legend, so strong and brave. They've got me feeling like a young stallion again. Whatever happens, we'll kill that beast."

Deica shook her head. "No, Grandpa, you won't. It's bigger than a house, it'll swallow all of you."

Grandpa laughed. "That's just your fear talking."

"No! I know! There are—What if there are more than one of them?"

He gave her a puzzled look. "What are you talking about?"

A different fear rose in her now, fear of being discovered. She didn't dare speak the truth. "I just meant—what if it kills you?"

He sighed. "We all live one life, Deica. And it always traces the same arc: ready, draw, release. My life has been drawn for a long time, longer than my son's, longer than…than your grandmother's. Maybe it's time for the snow to fall from my leaf."

"No! Don't die!" cried Deica stubbornly, beating her small fists against his chest.

"Hush, girl. Don't worry—no matter what, you'll be taken care of. I've spoken to Hiram and we're all agreed: you'll go to the priesthood." And he held her like a child, pressed against his gray-haired chest as she cried.

She knew then that she had to leave. The Worm was going to kill Grandpa and the other soldiers. And even if by some miracle they killed it instead, the best that would happen to her was that she would spend the rest of her life stuck in the same village in the middle of nowhere. Grandpa might be ready to end his days here, but her life was just getting started.

He'd said that there was no place for a two-legged freak girl in the city. But she could give herself a chance. She couldn't grow two more legs, but she could do something about being a girl.

That night, while the house slept, she did what she needed to do. Her hair first—she cut it and threw it into the forest so that no one would know. Then the clothes—a strap across her breasts to keep them tightly reined in, then she put on her tunic male-style, with her right arm bare and the belt tied low around her waist. With the muscles in her arm showing, no one would think her a girl. Finally, the packing—she took two old cloaks of Acrios' (one light and one heavy; both a little big but they would keep her warm), a jar of food from the pantry (some dried figs, bread and cheese, and the wild mushrooms she'd picked last week), a few things she might need to camp out (a knife, a blanket, a pot and cup, and flint to start a fire), and then, last and most important, her bow and arrows.

She set out before dawn. To avoid the village guard she started Outwards, into the forest, then circled back and caught the Inward road. With the sun rising, she turned toward the center of the Wheel and walked away from everything she'd ever known.

—— CHAPTER TWO ——
WHEN COWS TALK

It was exciting at first, to travel on her own, with all the Wheel in front of her and no one to tell her where to go or what to do. But the road was hard, and Deica soon found that the world didn't have much place for a penniless freak, whether boy or girl. She'd been hoping to trade work for food and lodging, but at every village she stopped they just stared at her two legs and told her to move on. Once, a bunch of teenagers started laughing and skipping stones down the road at her. She hurried on.

So Deica spent the nights outside, and slowly ate through her supplies. The bread and cheese and mushrooms went quickly; she tried to make the figs last as long as she could. A few days after she left she shot and roasted a squirrel, which filled her belly that night. But she lost three of her arrows before she finally brought it down. At that rate, she wouldn't have many meals left.

The nights were the hardest. No matter how tired she was from walking all day, when Deica lay on the cold ground with the noises of animals around her, she suddenly became wide awake. In the beginning she counted the stars and that helped, but after a few days the sky became overcast and the stars were hidden. What small fits of sleep she did manage to grab were broken by nightmares of Serpents chasing her.

The seventh day after she had set out from Delos was the worst, because the clouds finally opened up and started pouring down rain. The water soaked through both her cloaks, and her uncovered feet and legs were drenched and freezing. She knew that she could get sick or even die if she camped out in this weather, so she was determined to stay indoors even if she had to break in somewhere. But she was on a long stretch of empty road, and it was getting dark. As she walked the wind picked up, whipping the rain against her and roaring in her ears. Deica had never been more tired or cold or miserable in her life—it was all she could do just to put one foot in front of the other.

Suddenly, *whack!* Something big and bulky hit her from behind, and she went sprawling face down in the mud. Dazed, she raised her head, coughing out dirty water. She heard a deep "Whoa!" and the creaking of a wagon, then splashes in the mud as someone approached.

She struggled to push herself up. "A thousand apologies," said the voice. "I didn't see you." A strong arm reached down and pulled her to her feet. Deica turned toward the voice and saw a huge black bull.

No, not a bull, but the head of a bull. And the broad shoulders and beginning of a bull's back, but on top of a body with a chest and arms like a centaur, and two legs ending in great black hooves. The bull-creature was covered with a large wool cloak, clasped around the neck and nearly as soaked-through as Deica's.

As she turned to face him, the great hand released her and the creature stepped back in alarm. "Hoom...what sort of creature are you?" he asked.

Deica stumbled and tried to shake off her daze. "I'm a centaur," she said. "Who are you?"

The bull-creature looked her over doubtfully. "My name is Gustus. I am a merchant from the Kingdom of Minos. But you don't look like a centaur to me. In fact, I've traveled eight of the twelve kingdoms and never seen a creature like you. Are you one of the strange folk from the Wild Lands?"

"No, no, I'm a centaur. I was just born this way, with only two legs. And no tail. And feet instead of hooves."

Gustus said nothing, so Deica quickly added, "But whatever I am, I'm cold and tired and hungry. Do you know anywhere I could take shelter tonight?"

Gustus paused a long while. "Hoom. I think you had better come up with a better explanation of yourself before you run into someone more suspicious than I am. But it's plain that you're in a miserable state, and the Makers would not forgive me if I left you out on a night like this. There's an inn up the road, and space on my wagon to take you. It won't give you shelter, but my horses will make good time."

Deica looked at the horses for the first time. Even in the darkness and the rain she could tell that they were beautiful animals, young and strong. The largest one looked at Deica and cocked its head as though deciding what to make of her.

"Thank you," she said to Gustus. "I don't have much, but I owe you a debt of gratitude."

"I suppose one of the things you don't have is money for a room. But never mind, we'll cross that bridge when we come to it."

Gustus climbed to the top of his wagon and helped Deica up. "What's your name, lad?"

"Dei—uh, Deicos."

He raised an eyebrow. "Hoom. Pleased to meet you. Deicos."

Then Gustus reached into the wagon and pulled out a lantern, well wrapped in leather. With a few quick strokes he lit it, and put it out on a pole out in front of the wagon. "If there are any more strange creatures out tonight, let's try to see them before the horses run them over," he said with a smile. Then he urged on the horses, and they took off.

Deica huddled close to Gustus. She was still shivering and wet, but for the first time in days she had some hope.

After about an hour of riding through the downpour, they saw a light ahead, and as they drew up Deica could make out a large building with a stable in the back. It was marked with a picture of a fire—the sign of an inn—and another faded yellow picture of a hare.

Gustus pulled the wagon up and said, "Wait here," then climbed down and entered the inn. Deica waited on top of the wagon getting rained on for a few minutes, then moved under the overhang by the door.

Suddenly, the door burst open, nearly hitting her as Gustus walked past with a centaur boy behind him. Gustus talked so quickly that the boy hardly had time to look at her. "Make sure the horses are well fed. Carrots if you have them for Alethra—that's the big mare to your left—oats for the chestnut one, and dry straw for them all, and if the weather gets better a slice of peach."

The boy nodded as though he were following all this, and then looked around to where Deica was standing by the door. But Gustus broke in, distracting him, "Look here! Take good care of them and I'll make it worth your while." Gustus reached into his pouch and tossed several silver coins to the boy, who dropped them and scrambled to pick them up from the mud. "Quick, boy! The horses are getting wet!" roared Gustus, giving Deica a wink. The centaur boy jumped up in confusion and grabbed the reins, leading the horses off to the stable.

"Follow me," Gustus said to Deica, and went into the inn again.

Deica followed him into a large, warm room lit by a blazing fire. Dozens of centaurs were eating and drinking there, standing around tall tables in the center of the room or at the long bar to the side. Two satyrs sat in a corner. Deica could hear the room grow quiet and feel the weight of the stares as they entered.

Gustus lumbered towards the fire, then halfway across the room looked up in surprise. "Don't tell me you've never seen a young Bull-roar before," he said with a laugh. "This is my nephew, Deicos. His horns and hooves are just starting to grow out." Then he lowered his voice and added, "In fact, I'd be a bit careful with the stares if I were you. Our mating season is coming up and there's no telling who the young one might mistake for a cow."

At this comment, all the centaurs suddenly seemed to find other things in the room much more interesting to look at than Deica. The ones standing by the fire moved to a table. Even the two satyrs in the corner took one look at Deica, then looked at each other, then went back to their meal.

With the hearth to themselves, Deica and Gustus took off their cloaks and began to dry off. Gustus called to the innkeeper for dinner, then pulled a wooden table and chairs up to the fire. Deica felt the warmth from the fire and the stew slowly seep into her, warming her down to her bones.

"Ah," said Gustus. "A hot meal and a warm fire. Sometimes I think half the pleasure of traveling is stopping for the night, and if I were a saner man I'd take that pleasure at my own home instead of these country inns. But more's the pity, more's the pity."

The simple dinner of bread, stew, and wine was like heaven after the past week of going hungry. Deica ate her fill and more. Gustus consumed a vast amount, relishing every bite and swallow. When dinner was at an end, he leaned his great bulk back in his small chair and said: "Hoom. So, Deicos, welcome to the Golden Hare. Now you have food and shelter, which I am happy to provide as an act of charity. But I am a curious soul, and if as you say you feel indebted to me, then you could repay me with some truth about yourself.

"As for me, I am a simple Bullroar merchant. I take finished goods from the cities of Minos to the frontiers of Sagita, and furs and feathers back to Minos, along the way trading in the Goatfoot Forests, Kria, Zigos—wherever the markets take me. I'm too poor to own slaves or even a decent caravan, but my horses and cart serve well enough to provide for my family, and my wife is strong enough to keep the home in my absence.

"You, on the other hand, are quite mysterious. Apart from your strange physique, you are traveling alone and at night in wild country, carrying little baggage except for a weapon and apparently no money. Someone more suspicious than I might have raised the alarm on seeing you, especially with these recent Serpent attacks. For myself, I'm willing to trust you—but I'd like to know whom I'm trusting."

Gustus leaned forward, bringing his great bull's face close to hers, and said, "So what's your story?"

Deica hesitated. She had hardly talked to anyone since her grandmother had died, much less such a strange creature in such a strange place. But there was something about Gustus that made her feel safe. Slowly, hesitantly, she began to tell her story, from her birth

as a "freak" through the attack on Leucta, her flight from Delos, and the way that the centaurs on the road had rejected her. At times it was too much: she rushed past some parts, like her grandmother's death, for fear that she might start crying. And she kept one secret—that she was a girl.

Gustus watched her impassively, saying nothing. Finally she finished, "So...I can see that you've traveled a lot. Maybe you could tell me the best places to go." And she added suddenly, "Or maybe we could travel together," as though she'd just thought of it instead of hoping for it ever since he'd brought her here.

Gustus lowered his massive head. "By traveling together I take it you mean that I drive you around and pay for your food and lodging," he said. "Hoom. Do you have any skills?"

"I can shoot a bow," she said proudly.

"No doubt. But I don't need anything stuck with arrows at the moment. Anything else?"

"I can—" Deica caught herself. She'd been about to say: I can cook. I can clean. She could do lots of things that a centaur boy would never have been taught. "I can shoe horses," she said instead. Not exactly true, but she'd shod lots of centaurs. How much harder could it be?

Gustus frowned. "I'm a merchant, not a farrier." She didn't know what to say to that.

Finally he said, "Hoom. You probably won't survive on your own in this country, and I'm not going to leave you here. But I don't think you're telling me the whole truth. If you want to keep who and what you are a secret, that's your business. But if there's anything I need to know for my safety or yours, you'd better tell me now. If you've got enemies, I don't want them coming after you in the middle of the night and catching us unawares."

What an odd idea, Deica thought. "No, no, there's nothing like that."

"Hoom. Good." He seemed satisfied. "There is one thing you can do for me. Give me your hand."

"What?"

"Your hand, Deicos. Give me your hand." Gustus held out his own huge hand palm upwards on the table, his three thick and stubby fingers opposite an enormous thumb. Hesitantly, Deica stretched out her hand, and Gustus held it in his palm and examined it.

"Yes, that'll do," he said, letting her go. Seeing her confused look, he added, "It's this damn centaur money. Silver pennies half the width of my finger! May the Makers help me, I can hardly make change."

And so Deica became Gustus's moneychanger. The next morning the sky had cleared and she helped him set up his wagon in a muddy field outside the inn. Gustus sold a variety of metal goods, from simple iron pots and pans that might have been found in Deica's home to ornate doorknobs, patterned silverware, and finely-wrought knives and armor the likes of which she'd never seen.

The inn's guests and staff came by to browse, and Gustus had a pitch and an item for everyone. When he and the customer reached a price, he gave Deica a large iron moneybox and she took the customer's money.

It made Deica nervous to count the money with both Gustus and the customers watching, and she made a few mistakes. But Gustus helped her and didn't get angry. And sitting there in the afternoon sun, she couldn't help but feel a thrill. She'd done it. She'd left Delos and was traveling the Wheel, meeting new people and seeing strange sights in a place further from home than she'd ever been. She smiled from the inside out.

The day's take was three gold talents and sixty nine and a half silver pennies, more than Grandpa used to make from a month's crops. "Not a bad day, eh Deicos?" Gustus boomed. "Of course we'll do better in Kerigos."

Kerigos was the proper name for what Deica and her family had simply called "the city." Deica had never been there, but she'd heard amazing things about it: that it had a wall fifteen feet tall all around it, buildings made of stone instead of wood, and an outdoor market twice the size of Delos. Most importantly, she'd heard that even though it was a centaur city, people from every one of the Twelve Kingdoms lived there. She couldn't help but think that her own strange body would be better accepted.

So over the next week, as they traveled along the road to Kerigos, she grew more and more excited. She was already seeing new things every day: centaurs dressed in all kinds of colors and fabrics, Imperial coins stamped with an eagle instead of the King and his bow, a town with exotic furs and blankets in its marketplace in addition to the usual grains and vegetables. One day she even saw hundreds of centaur soldiers shining brightly in their armor marching down the road. They looked so splendid with their brightly colored standards and their great bows that she stared at them the whole time, even though Gustus pulled off the road to avoid them and insisted on sitting in front of her so she could hardly see.

The only bad thing that happened on the way to Kerigos was Alethra losing her shoe. Alethra was Gustus's largest mare, his pride and joy, so when he stopped for a rest and noticed that the shoe had come off her right rear hoof, he wanted to fix it right away.

Gustus took out a brand-new horseshoe that he kept in his cart for emergencies, and tossed it to Deica. Then he gave her a hammer and nails. "Here's another chance to be useful, Deicos," he boomed with a smile. "You said you'd done this before. Let's see you shoe this horse."

"Sure!" Deica cried loudly, trying to make up for her lack of experience with enthusiasm. "Just unhitch her and hold her by her...her head."

Deica had shod her grandfather many times. It was a simple process: Grandpa lifted his back leg, she moved the shoe around until he told her that the fit was right, and she hammered it in.

She touched Alethra's leg. "Here, girl," she said gently. "Give me your leg." Nothing happened.

"Give me your leg, Alethra," she said louder. "I've got to shoe you." Deica pulled harder on the leg, and Alethra took a step toward her, bringing her hoof down on Deica's bare foot. Deica screamed in pain; it felt like a mountain was on her foot. Alethra looked back casually. Gustus pulled the horse forward, and she lifted her hoof as she stepped away. "Ah! Ah! My foot!" cried Deica, dropping to the ground.

Gustus came over and examined her. There was a huge red hoof shape on her instep that was already starting to swell. He felt it tenderly, sending spasms of pain through her foot. "Looks like nothing's broken," he said.

The sharp pains faded, replaced by a dull ache. "All right. I can try again. I'll be more careful." She started to get up.

Gustus stopped her. "You've never done this before, have you?"

"Sure I have. Plenty of times. Well, I mean, with centaurs. I guess horses are a little harder to handle."

Gustus half-smiled. "Hoom. Just like someone else I know." He scooped her up in his giant arms. "Let's leave her shoeless for now," he said. "It's bad enough having one of you lame."

So Alethra went unshod until they reached the next town and found a farrier. Gustus had him show Deica how to get the horse's leg without getting stepped on, how to trim to hoof, and where to nail in the shoe to give it the best wear. Just as Deica had thought, it wasn't much different from centaurs.

And it seemed to Deica that afterwards, Alethra was easier to handle and happier to see her. Deica told Gustus that she thought Alethra was grateful that Deica had asked for her leg politely instead of just lifting it up like most people did. Gustus laughed.

"If you say so," he said. "But next time, don't try something you don't know how to do, all right?"

"How am I going to learn anything, then?" she asked. Gustus laughed again.

That night, they stayed at an inn only a few miles from the walls of the city. After they'd eaten and retired to their room, Gustus looked uncomfortable, and said to her awkwardly, "Deicos? There's something that I want to discuss with you."

"Yes?"

"Hoom. It's about your appearance. You know, out on the frontier people are a little more accepting of, ah, differences. But since we're going to be in Kerigos tomorrow, I was thinking that maybe you would want to wear some sort of disguise to look, well, more normal."

Deica was crushed. "A disguise?"

"Yes, you know, maybe something to make you look like a satyr—put some goat horns on your head and grow out your beard a little, something like that." Her disappointment must have showed, because Gustus quickly said, "Not if you don't want to, of course. Hoom. There's all kinds of people in this world, lad, and you shouldn't feel ashamed of being different. It's just that you might attract a lot of attention."

She shook her head. "I've spent my life hidden away. I want to be myself tomorrow."

Gustus looked disappointed, but he nodded and said, "I understand. But when we're in the city, just stay close to me and do what I tell you, all right?"

"Of course," she said, brightening up. "Don't I always?" Gustus looked like he was about to say something in reply, but thought the better of it.

So Deica entered Kerigos riding on Gustus's wagon, disguise-free except for looking like a boy. The city was amazing. Not only were the walls as tall as any building in her village, they were made of solid stone and were wide enough for a centaur to stand on. And the crowds!—she had never seen so many people, people everywhere, riding alone or in groups, pulling wagons with packages, carrying packs on their backs, walking and trotting up and down the streets. She stared open-mouthed at all the activity. Gustus looked at her amused. "If you think this is big," he said, "you should see the Imperial Capital. Roads twice as wide and buildings three times as tall. Most of them dating from the beginning of the Age, too."

Deica nodded dumbly, still trying to take everything in. The only disappointment was that almost everyone was a centaur. She also saw sheepheads—creatures with a body like hers but the head of a ram. But she'd seen those in Delos, including her own family's slave, Gesel. Gesel had once told her that there was a sheephead Kingdom where there were free sheepheads, but all of the ones Deica saw here were carrying large packs and following closely behind centaurs, so she guessed they were slaves.

Besides sheepheads and centaurs, there were a few satyrs, with goat legs and goat horns, walking through the streets leering at anything that moved. These seemed more common here than in Delos. Looking at them, Deica thought that it was probably a good idea that she didn't try to disguise herself as one. All the males had full beards and hairy bodies—she couldn't imagine that any disguise she could have managed would have fooled anyone.

"Is it true that all of the Twelve Races live here?" she asked Gustus.

Gustus shrugged. "I doubt you'd find merfolk in the river," he replied. "As for the rest—could be. I'm sure we'll see more in the marketplace—Whoa..."

The traffic suddenly stopped and Gustus reined in their horses. Four satyrs had moved into the crossroads ahead and blocked traffic to allow a clear path. Behind them was a unicorn.

A unicorn. Deica had heard of them, but nothing could prepare her for seeing one in person. With its pearly white coat, golden mane, and bright diamond horn, it shone like a creature from the heavens, like a star itself. It practically glided across the road, its head high, its hooves barely touching the ground. It was the most beautiful creature Deica had ever seen.

The unicorn had followers. In addition to the four satyrs clearing the way, three small monkeys scurried at its feet, each with a small golden-backed brush that they used to brush the unicorn's legs and coat as it walked. They were quite skilled at what they did, quickly darting in and out of its legs without missing a stroke or getting stepped on. Finally, behind the unicorn walked two large orangutans, huge apes with arms stretching to the ground. One of them looked back and forth through the crowd, as though watching for some unknown threat. The other looked straight ahead, and carried an enormous metal chest on its back.

When the unicorn passed and traffic began to move again, she took a deep breath and turned to Gustus. He was staring after it.

"Wow," he said. "Did you see the size of that moneybox?"

"The moneybox?" exclaimed Deica.

He looked back at her, and said, "Hoom. Ah, yes, first time you'd seen a Virgin, was it? Beautiful creatures, just beautiful. A pity their personalities don't match."

Deica wanted to ask Gustus what he meant, but he seemed impatient to move on, so she said nothing.

The marketplace was a huge outdoor square filled with rows of carts and booths where merchants sold wares of every type and quality. They passed wine shops run by satyrs, stuffed figs and medicinal wares sold by centaurs, decorative sea-shells owned by what looked like a free sheephead, and many, many more. Deica hardly had time to take it in as Gustus made a beeline for an empty space to set up their stall.

Several strange creatures were crawling on a wagon in the space next to theirs. They had a head and chest like Deica's, but below the waist their bodies were like giant scorpions: black and segmented, with eight small legs growing out of their sides and a curved, segmented tail ending in a nasty stinger. Instead of hands, they had pincer-like scorpion claws. Deica had heard of these creatures, too. In the Scarpi wars before she was born, they had killed her father.

Deica looked at Gustus anxiously. "Aren't those..." she searched for the right word: "...enemies?"

"Ah, the Scarpi aren't a bad lot," replied Gustus. "Just don't piss them off; they'll kill you in a heartbeat."

Not very reassured, Deica looked back at the Scarpi. Six of them, four small and two large, scuttled around their wagon, unpacking bundles and opening them up. They seemed to be hanging up woven rugs, placemats, and other small crafts for sale. The two large ones—the parents?—were directing the others. The largest one eyed Deica curiously. "He-iy Goostoos," he said. "Who e-iss the little-uh one?"

Deica shrank behind Gustus. Gustus replied, "My new assistant, Deicos. He's shy. How's business, Parabakina?"

Gustus went over to talk to the Scarpi while Deica set up the cart. They seemed to know each other well—Gustus even spoke some of their language—so Deica decided that Gustus must have been joking earlier.

When Gustus came back to help her set up, he looked worried. "Parabakina says that the attacks on the frontier are getting worse," he said. "They think there's more than one Serpent involved now, and maybe even some coordination of their attacks. Everyone's nervous. It's bad for business."

Deica looked down. She didn't want to think about this.

Gustus bent down so that his face was level with hers. "I asked him if there was news from Delos," he said. "He hadn't heard."

"It doesn't matter," she said, still looking away. "I'm never going back there anyway."

But she couldn't help thinking of her grandfather, and she fidgeted as she set up Gustus's stall. She tried to use the sights and sounds of the market to turn her mind from thoughts of Serpents. She saw some strange creatures dressed in metal plate armor, standing on two legs but with the heads of lions. They were so tall and erect, they looked like kings.

Deica pointed those out to Gustus. "Hoom, yes," he said gloomily. "Sinhar. They go where the wars are."

Deica didn't talk much to Gustus after that. Her job changing money was much as it was in the outer towns, and she'd practiced enough that it was easy now. So she spent most of the day just watching and working and trying not to think about the past.

Then, late in the afternoon, she saw him. He was facing her with his back to another merchant's booth a little ways away. He was older, maybe in his late forties, tall and balding, with his knees slightly bent as though he was leaning back against something. But he had two legs, two arms, and a head...just like hers! She'd never seen anyone who looked like her before. People walked by him without staring.

Deica turned to Gustus excitedly. "Gustus, who is—"

"In a minute," Gustus said gruffly, deep in conversation with a customer. She looked back at the man, but now a train of wagons had come between them and she couldn't see him anymore. Had he started walking away? There were so many people here; if he left she was sure she'd never find him again.

Deica took one look back at Gustus, then slipped from the stall and ran toward the man. She moved down the lane on the side of a fig cart, hidden from view by the wagon and horses, taking sidelong glances through the wheels. But when she got to the stall, there was no one there.

Quickly she looked around, and spied him just as he turned a corner, strangely still facing her, as though he were walking backward. She raced down the street, weaving between centaurs, desperate to reach him.

Just as she turned the corner, an iron hand gripped her shoulder. "Witchling!" hissed a voice. Deica was spun around roughly to face an old, strong satyr with a wild grey beard and menacing horns. His face was an angry scowl, and his eyes stabbed her like daggers. "Fetch the guard!" he bellowed into her face. "I've caught a spy!"

A few centaurs ran off. Others looked up and a crowd began to gather. The satyr's nails dug into her skin. "I've seen your kind in the Wild Lands," he said harshly. "You're here to spy on us, aren't you?"

Before she had a chance to say anything, another voice spoke—a smoother, softer voice. "Excuse me, my goatfooted friend. May I be of assistance?" Deica turned to see the man that she'd been following.

He was middle-aged and thin, neatly dressed with distinguished gray hair and a clean-shaven face.

The man looked at her and his eyes widened. Then he *spun*—a quick, disorienting motion—and suddenly another man stood in front of her. He also had two legs and two arms, but a shorter, heavier build with a wider face. Deica peered around and saw that the two men were joined at the buttocks and the upper back. What she had thought was a creature like her was actually two bodies joined together back to back, making a single creature with four legs, four arms, and two heads.

The shorter half of the creature looked at Deica in disbelief. "I'll be damned!" he whispered. "A Single."

"This is no business of yours, Twin," growled the satyr, pulling her away. "I've seen creatures like this before, witchlings from the Wild Lands. They come out in the dark, crawling out of the earth like worms and casting their foul spells on the innocent." The crowd began murmuring among themselves.

The shorter half of the Twin snorted and said, "Yes, and after a long night of drinking I bet you've also seen pigs fly and elephants dance. Let him go and get out of the way, idiot."

Suddenly, the crowd parted, and three large centaurs rode up. Broad-shouldered and tall, they towered over the Twin, the satyr, and far above Deica. They wore coats of tough leather, with clubs at their left side and swords at their right.

"Hold, citizens!" the tallest one called. "I am Drycas, Captain of the Market." Then he addressed the satyr. "What's going on, Oenydon?"

"I caught this *thing* sneaking around the market," said the satyr, pushing Deica in front of him but still keeping a grip on her shoulder. "You can see for yourself that it is not of the Makerite races. It is a witchling, come from the Wild Lands to spy on us!"

Drycas regarded Deica doubtfully. "Who are you? And what do you say to this?"

Deica swallowed hard. "I'm Deicos. I'm not a spy. I was just following him," she said, pointing to the Twin, "because he looks like me."

Drycas glanced at the Twin. The Twin spun around again and with his taller, thinner half facing Deica, bowed and said, "Delighted to meet you, sir." Then he turned to Drycas. "Good Captain, miraculous to behold, this young man has the form of a Single, the very form that the Makers wore when they walked the Wheel two thousand years ago. This lad's appearance is an omen of great favor. I have no doubt that he is innocent of any wrongdoing."

Meanwhile, the Twin's shorter half whispered to Deica, "Follow my lead. I'll get you out of this."

"Two-face!" snarled the satyr. "What do you know? It is a witchling, I tell you!" His eyes bulged and sweat glistened on his forehead, only inches from Deica's face. Deica trembled in fear. The crowd muttered in agreement.

"Calm down, Oenydon. I'll handle this," said the captain.

"I suggest you remove the goatfoot, captain. He's disturbing the peace," said the Twin's taller half.

"Quiet! Or I'll remove *you*," snapped the captain. Both halves of the Twin stared at him, speechless.

The captain turned to Deica. "What's your business in the market?"

She hesitated. She didn't want to get Gustus in trouble.

"Well? Speak up! Why are you here?"

"I...I came to sell things," she stammered.

"You're a merchant?" Drycas frowned in disbelief. "Where is your cart? Where are your wares?"

This was all her fault for going off on her own. But she wouldn't make it worse for Gustus. She looked at the ground and said nothing.

The satyr Oenydon laughed loudly and picked her up, showing her to the crowd. "Look at it! See how it lies! Has anyone seen a creature like this? It is the kin of dragons, here to breach the city walls!" Deica flushed with fear and shame, caught in the centaurs' angry stares. Oenydon swayed as he held her and his eyes were glazed as though he was drunk, but his voice had a rough intensity that caught the crowd alight.

"Oenydon is right!" cried some.

"Yes, it is a spy!"

"Good people, I'm sure that there is a reasonable explanation—" began the Twin.

"Shut up!"

"Stupid Twin! Get out of the way!"

"Order!" shouted Captain Drycas. "I'll handle this."

But Oenydon roared, "This is beyond you, Drycas! To the High Priest with him! Give him the Test of Truth!" His eyes were fiery and his face red and twisted. He seemed to have some strange power over the crowd. They surged forward and roared, "Yes! Yes! To the high priest!"

The Captain and his guards were jostled. The Twin was pushed into Oenydon and Deica; his elbow knocked into her ribs. The Twin's thin face looked panicked, but his stockier half had an angry frown. He pushed back against the centaurs. The crowd yelled louder: "To the High Priest!"

"Yes, the Test of Truth!"

"And then the sacrifice!"

"Yes, the sacrifice!"

The *sacrifice?* Deica looked desperately at Captain Drycas. But the guards seemed to have accepted the crowd's verdict. One of them grabbed Deica roughly and pulled her out of Oenydon's grasp. "All right! To the High Priest! Now move aside!" called Captain Drycas.

Drycas and the guard who wasn't holding Deica took out their wooden clubs and began elbowing and knocking their way through the crowd. The centaurs gave way, though they fell in behind Deica in a mass, still shouting.

"To the high priest!"

"Sacrifice the spy!"

Deica looked back, terrified, half-hoping to see Gustus in the crowd, but the only thing her eyes could find was the red face of Oenydon, lips twisted in a maniacal grin, horns glistening in the afternoon heat.

—— CHAPTER THREE ——

THE HIGH PRIEST

The journey to the High Priest was rough and short. The centaur guards half-carried and half-dragged Deica while the crowd followed behind. She could see the Twin running along with them, calling vainly for the guards to slow down. She felt alone and afraid.

But when they reached the Temple, Deica's fear turned to awe. She had expected something like the temple in Delos—an altar at the bottom of a hill with some stone benches on the hillside. But this was a huge building with a rising roof and two towers fifty feet high, each capped by a tremendous golden bell. The doors were twelve feet tall and made of ornately carved wood; the walls were pale white stone. It was like nothing she'd ever seen.

But she had no time to stare, as the centaurs pulled her quickly inside and closed the doors. They exchanged a few words with a black-haired, dark-faced satyr, and then sat her down on a narrow wooden bench. The satyr opened an inner door and went further into the Temple.

She waited a long time, hearing the dull roar of the crowd outside—like a great beast circling the Temple—and the voices of Captain Drycas and others addressing it sternly. She couldn't make out what they said. Her guards paced back and forth uncomfortably, tapping their hooves on the stone floor. After a while, the outer doors swung open again, and the Twin appeared in the doorway.

"A pleasure to see you again, Deicos," said the Twin's taller half. "Good news! The crowd is dispersing, and Captain Drycas has graciously allowed me to speak with you."

Then he spun around. "Don't worry; we'll get you out of here," said his shorter half.

"What's going to happen to me?" asked Deica.

"You're going to see the High Priest. He's what passes for a leader out here in the country."

The country? Deica let it pass. "What will he do?"

"Question you, I assume. They mentioned some kind of test. But I'll take care of it. Just let me do the talking."

"What did they mean by a sacrifice?"

The Twin looked uncomfortable, started to answer, coughed, and then spun, so that his taller half was again facing Deica. "Nothing to worry about, nothing at all," he said, awkwardly patting Deica's arm. "I'm sure that the High Priest is a reasonable fellow and will have nothing to do with such, such—*barbarism* as Makerite sacrifice."

Deica's mind flashed back to the crazed look in Oenydon's eyes and the noise of the crowd yelling for her blood. She felt sick.

"I understand that this is an awkward moment for us to meet," the Twin continued. "But allow me to introduce myself. I am Betramal. My other half is Betramos. You're also welcome to address either of us as Betram—or both of us for that matter—which often makes the matter of address simpler when you don't need to distinguish one from the other."

This was making her head hurt. Betramal continued, "We are the Diplomatic Representative of the Senate of the Twin Cities to the city of Kerigos, and all of this outer region I might add, although the outer region is not officially included in our title due to an oversight, the details of which I need not describe, but suffice it to say—"

But Deica never heard what Betramal was going to say next, because at that moment the door leading into the Temple opened, and the black-haired satyr guard walked out, grim-faced and bearing a long wooden stick. He jabbed the stick in the air at Deica and said to the others, "The High Priest will see him. Alone."

The centaurs stepped aside, seemingly relieved not to be coming. Betramos said angrily, "That's not right!" but he did nothing as the satyr ignored him, pulled Deica up by the wrist, and dragged her inside. The satyr led her down a wide hallway to a large double door.

Then he opened the door, pushed her inside, and slammed it behind her with a hollow thud.

The first thing she noticed was the candles, thousands of them lighting up the room—small ones against the walls, larger ones lining a path between white stone benches, huge ones in glass holders around the altar. Among them scurried dark creatures, small and hairy, which disappeared into crevices in the walls as she entered.

Then she heard the Voice—pure as glass, beautiful and unwavering. Somehow, it didn't break the silence of the room—it spoke to her from inside her mind. *Come here*, it said.

And then she saw the unicorn, standing behind the smooth stone altar. In the streets of the city he had been merely beautiful, here in the light of a thousand candles he shone like a god. She raised her hands to ward off the light reflecting from his coat and golden mane.

The Voice spoke again: *Come here, Deicos.* A chill of fear ran through her. Almost against her will, she began walking down the white carpet to the altar.

Do you know why you're here, Deicos?

Why she was here? What did he mean? She shook her head dumbly.

They want me to sacrifice you. They say that you are a spy and that you have blasphemed by claiming to be a Maker.

Horrified, she cried out, "No, no, I never—" but the Voice cut her off: *Hush*, and she suddenly realized how loud her voice had sounded in the stillness of the room. *There is no need to speak*, said the Voice. *Soon I will know your every thought.* And then the light of the candles dimmed, and the unicorn himself began to glow.

There is great power in the sacrifice of a thinking creature, continued the Voice. *Yet it is wrong to take such a life, unless the creature is evil beyond redemption.* The unicorn looked her in the eyes. *Are you evil, Deicos?*

41

In the unicorn's gaze Deica felt suddenly unclean, as though it was shining a light on all the bad things she'd ever done. She thought of how she'd abandoned her family when they were in mortal danger, and lied to everyone she'd met about who she really was, and broken her promise to Gustus, running off and leaving him. She turned her eyes away but kept walking down the path.

The unicorn moved around the altar, so gracefully that it seemed to be floating. *Many know darkness, Deicos. Many choose the path of lies some of the time. But in a few the root of evil runs much deeper. It grows like a cancer from their earliest years, until their hearts are black with bile and their very bones warped with malice. Do you know what I mean, Deicos?*

Each time he spoke the name "Deicos" it reminded her of her lies. Now she realized how much she'd hated her sister Anisa. And her mother, who gave her life, who fed her and clothed her and put up with her deformity—Deica had hated her too. She felt sick with guilt.

And there was something else, the thing she'd never told any-one, when she was nine years old and the Wild Forest had called to her. The forest was an evil place, everyone knew that. But she had followed its song. And she had seen them there—the Wild Folk, the Children of the Serpent. And they had—

We are not like other races, Deicos, said the Voice. Deica reached the altar, still averting her eyes. The candles were very dim now, and the unicorn was filled with a bright light concentrated in his horn. *The Makers created the others from dirt, the same dirt that gave birth to the Children of the Serpent. But the Makers made the Virgin race, the unicorns, from pure starlight. And so we are the purest of all, and blessed with the light of truth to use against the Serpent. So says the Book of Prayer: Lo! I send you the Light of the Wheel. And the Light shines in the darkness, for the Light is Truth, which no evil can withstand.*

The unicorn's horn shone like a sword of light, beautiful and terrible. Deica felt overwhelmed by her own evil. He circled her,

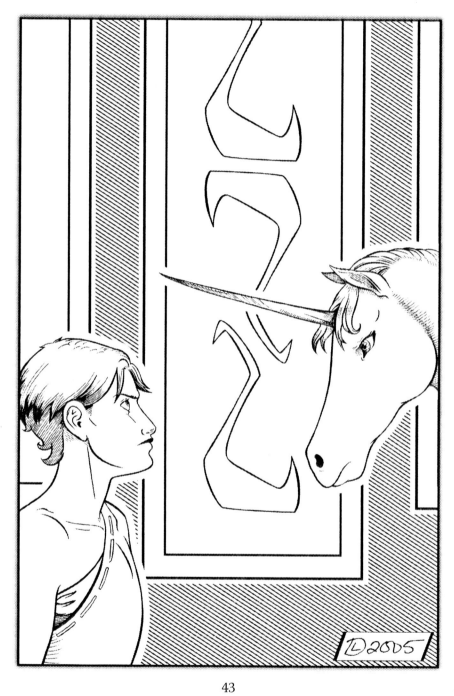

backing her up against the altar. His Voice grew softer. *I can see the suffering in your soul, Deicos. I can feel the pain that darkness has brought you. The light can burn it away. Face the truth, Deicos, and it will set you free.*

Free? Could she really be free of her sin? She gazed into the light. Yes, that was it—the way out, the ray of hope. She had been living a life of lies, but if she confessed it all, she could be good again. The unicorn was good. He was showing her the way.

But at the same time she heard another voice inside her mind, the voice of her own thoughts. It said, *This is magic. He's casting a spell on me.* She hesitated.

The unicorn lowered his head, his horn inches from her heart, burning her eyes like a white fire. *Do you have something to tell me, Deicos?*

He was trying to trick her, she thought, trying to make her think that she was evil. Looking up into his eyes, she said, "I'm innocent. I'm not a spy. I'm a good person."

The unicorn's eyes narrowed and she heard his Voice echo in her mind again, colder than before, judging her and finding her wanting. *Even now you resist the truth. Do you think you can hide from me? I tell you solemnly: everything you are will be revealed.* And he touched her heart with his horn.

Deica's body was suddenly filled with light, flowing like a river of energy from her heart outwards to the ends of her fingers and toes, shining on the dark corners of herself, dazzling her, revealing a world of images and sounds, memories and thoughts, wild fears and strange dreams, so much that she cried out in wonder. She couldn't describe or remember everything she saw, but beheld the whole of herself in an instant, like a wide valley lit up in a flash of lightning. And one thing was clear: it was beautiful. She was beautiful.

The High Priest jumped back, shutting off the light. Deica stared at him, dizzy, and he looked back in terror. Then he turned and galloped out of the room, crashing through the doors and into the hallway beyond, moving faster than she'd ever seen a creature move.

Deica felt lightheaded. She looked around. The room looked smaller than before. It was all white stone and glass, richly decorated, but now that the High Priest was gone the lighting was more ordinary. There was no one else in the room.

She walked back up the pathway, unusually aware of all her movements, as though her body were more alive. It was a good feeling.

The doors were splintered and broken where the High Priest's hooves and horn had hit them at full speed, and there was blood on the doors and in the hallway. She walked back the way she had come.

People were gathered in the entryway. Light was streaming in from the open Temple doors. The black-haired satyr was hopping nervously from one hoof to the other. The centaur guards were standing to the side looking uncomfortable. Betram, the Twin, was scratching both his heads. Drycas, the guard captain, was talking to someone else she knew—Gustus!

As soon as she entered they rushed forward.

"Are you all right?" asked Gustus.

"What happened? We saw the High Priest run out in a terrible hurry," said Betramal.

"Yes, where did he go?" asked Captain Drycas.

Still relishing her happy, alive feeling, Deica smiled and said, "I'm all right. I don't know where he went. He just touched me with his horn and then ran away."

"Did he say—uh, did he say what we should do with you?" asked the satyr.

"No, he didn't say anything about that."

The satyr looked like he wasn't used to this at all. He glanced outside as though looking for an escape route, and then said, "Wait— wait here. I'll find the Low Priest," and ran outside.

There was a long pause. Betramal said, "Well, you see, I told you that the High Priest would be..." and his voice trailed off as he finished, "...reasonable."

"It's good to see you well, lad," boomed Gustus, putting his huge arm around her. Then he addressed Drycas: "So, since the High Priest apparently has nothing to say against Deicos, I assume he is free to go."

Captain Drycas frowned. "Why didn't you tell me that you worked for Gustus?" he asked Deica.

"I didn't want to get him in trouble."

"Hmpf. If you had spoken up, we could have cleared this up back at the market. Now the priests are involved, and it's not so simple."

Betramal said, "Captain, this has gone past far enough. Deicos has done nothing wrong. I assure you that if he continues to be held unjustly, I will take this matter up to the highest authorities. As the civil officer here, you are answerable to the King and his governor, not to the High Priest."

Captain Drycas looked pained and said, "All right, all right, keep your shoes on." Then he said to Deicos, "I don't believe you're a spy. Gustus vouches for you, and I know him and trust him. But I can't just let you wander around and risk the crowd getting stirred up again.

"You're free to go if you agree to leave Kerigos and never come back. Otherwise, I'll have to put you in the keeping of the Low Priest."

"Who's the Low Priest?"

"You've met him. His name is Oenydon."

Deica shuddered. "Hoom," said Gustus. "Leaving the city will be no problem. In fact, we'll leave the entire kingdom of Sagita behind us. And believe me, we'll take great heed not to stand out. From now on, Deicos will dress in a heavy cloak to conceal any, ah, unusual features, and we'll steer clear of anyone who might notice that he's not completely normal."

Betramal shook his head in disbelief, then he spun around and Betramos said, "Are you crazy? Deicos is a Single, the first in centuries! We should be shouting his name from the rooftops, not hiding him away."

"Singles are a Twin legend," said Gustus. "The beliefs of other races may be more dangerous."

"More dangerous to whom? To Deicos, or to the Bullroar King?"

Gustus gave Betramos a cold look and said nothing.

"Well, Bullroar?" said Betramos. "Who are you really trying to protect: Deicos, or the race who wants him dead?"

"What's he talking about? Who wants me dead?" Deica asked Gustus.

"No one wants you dead. What happened in Minos twenty years ago has nothing to do with you."

"Oh. Well...what happened in Minos twenty years ago?"

"Yes, tell us all," said Betramos. "And tell us whose side you were on."

Gustus sighed. He sat down on the narrow bench, so small it hardly supported his bulk. "All right," he said. "All right."

Then he began: "Deicos, what were you taught about the Makers? What do you think they look like?"

"Well, they're supposed to be like balls of light, like the stars, only they can come invisibly and help you too. But sometimes I think of them as being like my grandmother, a kind of big old centaur that lives in the sky."

"But what about when they were on the Wheel, the old Maker heroes like Aeneas and Agnus? What form did they take then?"

"Oh. They were centaurs...weren't they?"

Gustus smiled. "Each race believes differently. In Minos, we're taught that Aeneas and his Maker army took the form of Bullroars. This is what all our literature says, and our oldest art and legends.

"When I was a young lad, perhaps no older than yourself, one of our leading scholars—his name was Epiphaxys—challenged this belief. He claimed that the Makers had neither bull's head nor hooves, that instead they looked something like you. He convinced a few people and even claimed to have found a child born to Bullroars who had

47

this strange form. This caused quite a stir. Many people wondered what it meant; some oracles called it the sign of a new Age.

"But King Niros didn't like it. So he beheaded Epiphaxys, and jailed and beat his followers, and outlawed any challenge to the doctrine. The child disappeared. Many didn't agree with this, but no one could stop King Niros. Everyone was afraid of him because he was the King.

"This is a lesson that my family knows well, because, you see, Epiphaxys was my father's brother." Gustus's voice grew hoarse. "He and two of my other uncles were killed, my father was put in prison, and we were all arrested. I was young, and they had no evidence against me, so I got off lightly.

"Deicos, I don't know if this has anything to do with you. But I do know that the world is a dangerous place, and being different makes it more so. Sometimes it's not wise to shout out your difference for all the Wheel to see. And I'm not saying that to protect King Niros." He cast a disapproving eye at Betramos. "I'm saying it to protect you."

"That was why you were so surprised when you saw me by the road," said Deica. "But you still picked me up." She smiled at him.

Gustus shrugged. "I couldn't just leave you there."

Betramos spun, revealing Betramal, who gave a small bow to Gustus and said: "Please forgive my twin for questioning your intentions. Betramos can be quick to judge. But I can see that you are an honorable Bullroar."

Then he said to Deica: "A story like this, on top of everything that happened to you today, must seem horrifying. And I can only imagine what other horrors you must have gone through growing up among these—" he paused as Captain Drycas glared at him, "ah, in this remote locale, shall we say. But please believe me: there are places in the Wheel not ruled by fear and violence.

"My home, the Twin Cities, is a land of freedom and equality. We have no King; our laws are written by an elected Senate, made up of wise men and scholars. We debate ideas freely and peacefully, and prize Truth above all. Careful study of history has convinced us that the Makers took the form of Singles, a form very like your own, and no educated person in the Twin Cities believes otherwise.

"Come with me to the Twin Cities, Deicos. You'll be a hero to the people who know what you really are. Along the way we can visit the Imperial Capital, the center of the entire Wheel, where Twins are honored as judges and teachers. I'm sure that the Prime Minister will want to meet you, perhaps even the Emperor himself."

Deica turned to Gustus. "Is this true? Would I be safer in the Twin Cities?"

Gustus looked at the ground gloomily. "Hoom. Maybe. Yes, maybe. But politics is a dangerous game. There wasn't any law against what my uncle did, either, until they killed him for it. You can still come with me, lad. We'll go to some of the same places, just more carefully."

Deica looked between Gustus and Betramal. Gustus had been her friend and protector, and she trusted him more than anything. But she couldn't hide anymore.

"I'm sorry," she said to Gustus, with tears in her eyes. "But I have to go with Betram."

Betramal clapped his hands. "Excellent. I'll fetch my carriage immediately, and meet you outside within the hour." And he ran off with an awkward gallop.

Gustus gave her a great bull-hug. "I only want the best for you, Deicos," he said. "I'll get your things and meet you out front." And he left.

She stepped outside with Captain Drycas and his two guards and waited. After a while Gustus rode up on Alethra, his largest horse, with her bow and pack.

"Take Alethra," he said. "She's always liked you. If you're ever in danger, she'll bear you swiftly away."

Deica couldn't believe it. Alethra must be worth twenty talents, as much as a good slave. She protested, but Gustus just shook his head and put Alethra's reins in her hand. Alethra nudged Deica with her nose.

Soon a large closed coach pulled up, driven by a sheephead slave and pulled by eight horses. Two heads poked out the window: Betramal and Betramos. "Ready to go?" asked Betramos.

"Stay out of Minos," Gustus said to her. "But if you ever need me, send a message to my house on the Fifth Hill in the city of Adrix."

Deica gave Gustus one last hug. "Thank you for everything."

"May the Makers be with you," he replied. Then he added, in a voice too low for Betram or Drycas to hear: "...girl."

She stared at him. How long had he known?

But there was no time to ask. Gustus lifted Deica onto her horse and she rode off, following Betram's coach. She glanced back at Gustus as he faded from view next to the Temple, then she faced forward and raced on, through the gates of Kerigos and Inward to the center of the Wheel.

—— CHAPTER FOUR ——

MASQUERADE

A few minutes after they rode out of the city, Betramal stuck his head out of the coach window. "Would you care to join us?" he called. "Perhaps you'd be more comfortable inside."

It was a beautiful day on a straight and easy road, and Deica was enjoying the ride. "No thanks," she said. "I'm fine."

Betramos laughed, and his head replaced Betramal's in the window. "I think my twin meant that we have a lot to talk about. And that it'll be easier to talk if we're not shouting through the window."

Enjoyment and curiosity battled inside Deica, and curiosity won. She pulled up and let the driver hook Alethra to his team, then climbed into the coach. The inside was rich and luxurious, with dark-paneled walls and black leather seats so smooth she felt like she was sliding off of them. It was strange to be in such a rich coach, but she felt a secret thrill. All her life her two-legged body had brought her misery. Now maybe it was leading her to something good.

Betramos drew the velvet curtains closed, and the coach became dark and cool as a cave. "I think it's time we begin your education," he said.

For the rest of the day she talked to Betram or, more accurately, he talked to her. She'd never met anyone who talked as much as he did; Betramal, his taller half, was especially prone to lengthy monologues about obscure theories of philosophy or history. Betramos talked more simply and about more practical things, but he had lots to say, too. Most of their references she didn't know, and half the words were in Imperial. She made herself exhausted just trying to follow it all.

But what she did understand was fascinating. He told her that Sagita, the kingdom of centaurs, was only one kingdom among twelve, and a small and backward one at that. He described all the other kingdoms, telling her about the Emerald Sea, where the half-fish merfolk live underwater, the bright beaches of Kria where the sheepheads come from, the unicorns who live in the Virgin Wood but serve as priests throughout the Wheel, and the wild Goatfeet—the satyrs—who serve under them.

Deica interrupted. "Why did the unicorn in Kerigos run away from me? If he's a priest, wouldn't he know I'm good?"

Betramos looked vaguely annoyed and spun around. Betramal cleared his throat and said, "Hm. Yes, well, you see, despite their high status and position, Virgins are actually quite superstitious, prone to flights of fancy, one might even say irrational. So seen in that light, his behavior is—in a manner of speaking—perfectly clear." Deica guessed that that meant Betram didn't know.

Betram continued, teaching her about the Scarpi (half-scorpion barbarians who live in the desert), the Zigots (strange creatures made of wood and metal), the brave Sinhar, the mysterious Mistfolk, the reclusive Carob Islanders, and the Bullroars, who work the metal of their mountains and travel the Wheel to trade it. ("Like Gustus!" exclaimed Deica. "Yes, yes, quiet now," said Betramal.)

But most of all, he told her about the Twins and their land, the Twin Cities, on the other side of the Wheel. The Twins were the keepers of education and culture for the entire Wheel, he said—the judges, teachers, and ministers for all the major cities in the Twelve Kingdoms, especially the Imperial Capital. He told her how the Twin Cities have been the most peaceful and advanced of the Twelve Kingdoms for centuries, and how the Twins live now only to bring the light of civilization to the other races, to uplift the entire Wheel.

By the time the sun set, Deica's head was spinning. That night she dreamed she rode Alethra through a great city filled with throngs of cheering people, every one of them different from the other, all freaks like her, and all throwing flowers at her feet. She woke eager to hear more, and the next day Betram continued where he'd left off.

So it went for weeks: Alethra was hooked to the team and Deica rode in the coach and tried to absorb "what every civilized child ought to know" as Betram put it. They made good time as they traveled Inward on the white cobblestone Milk Roads (built by Aeneas at the dawn of the Age, Betramal told her), heading toward the Imperial Capital (the home of the Emperor who rules all of the Twelve Kingdoms, Betramos said).

Deica was grateful for the chance to learn something, which she'd never had back home, but after a while she couldn't help wanting a little real-world experience to go along with it. As the weeks went by, the cities they stopped in grew larger and the sights stranger, but each night Betram hurried her secretly into their inn as though he were afraid of someone seeing her. This wasn't exactly what she had in mind when he'd told her that her name should be "shouted from the rooftops." So one night she said so.

"Ah, well, I understand, Deicos, I understand," answered Betramal. "Of course you'll see all that I promised you: great cities, all the Twelve Races, everything, once we get to the Capital. But until then, for your own safety it's better not to show yourself."

"Why?"

"Well, surely you remember what happened in Kerigos," he said. "Barbaric, simply barbaric, the way those centaurs called for your blood. Why, if I hadn't stepped in and calmed them down, who knows what might have happened, hm? No, no, much better to wait till we're out of centaur lands.

"But I'll tell you what: I have an appointment with the Regional Minister tomorrow morning. Suppose I take you with me? That's an exciting change of pace, isn't it? Not everyone gets a chance to meet the Regional Minister!"

Meeting the Regional Minister didn't sound like much fun to Deica, but she agreed to go along. The Regional Minister turned out to be a Twin, a superior of Betram's. Betram told him how he'd heroically rescued Deica from a rioting mob and rode out of town with the centaurs hot on their heels. The Minister asked Betram lots of questions about Deica as though she weren't there. When he finally addressed her he spoke very slowly, like he was talking to an idiot. Deica didn't say much.

After that day two Twin guards traveled with them, one riding on each side of the coach. Betram explained that the Regional Ministry of the Twin Cities had sent them for her protection.

"Why is it so dangerous?" Deica asked. "We're farther Inward now. I thought you said that the educated people in the big cities would like me."

"We-ll, yes," said Betramos. "Here in Inner Sagita you might be accepted. But think about the politics of it. Here you are, a Single, someone holy and important for the entire Wheel. But the centaurs didn't exactly honor you, did they? Not only didn't they recognize you, they accused you of being a spy and nearly sacrificed you. If that became known, it would be very embarrassing for the Centaur King. And believe me he wouldn't hesitate to hurt you or even kill you to prevent that. You grew up among centaurs, you must know how violent they can be."

Deica didn't say anything, but she couldn't agree. It was true that some centaurs had hurt her, but her grandfather and grandmother had been kind, and they were centaurs too. Besides, she'd always felt like a centaur herself, even though she was different. Maybe she looked more like a "Single" or half of a Twin, but she didn't feel like one.

The next few days Deica was so gloomy she could hardly concentrate on her studies. She needed to ride, and she felt like practicing archery too. Betram kept saying, "Just a little longer. We'll be safe soon."

Then one night they stepped out of the coach onto the road, and in the light of the setting sun she saw the largest castle she'd ever seen. Built on a hill at the top of the city, it was marked by a huge tower rising up to the sky, and on it flew a great flag of a golden bow—the symbol of the Centaur King!

"Is that the Royal Palace?" she asked Betram excitedly.

Betramos smiled. "Yes it is, Deicos. We're in Chiron, the capital of Sagita. And I've got good news: tomorrow is the moment you've been waiting for, your grand coming-out."

She stared. "Will I—Will I meet the King?"

Betramos coughed and spun so that Betramal was facing her. "Er, no, not the King. But you'll meet lots of others: ministers, poets, judges, all manner of cultural and political leaders."

"At the Palace?" she asked, confused.

"Ah...hmm, no, not at the Palace—at the residence of the Twin Ambassador to Sagita. You'll meet the Ambassador himself tomorrow morning, and then your presence will be announced at a great banquet tomorrow evening. You see, the residence of the Ambassador is technically not a part of Sagita, and therefore not subject to the rule of the Centaur King. Thus we'll present you in full view of all the Sagitan nobility, but they won't be able to do a thing about it. Brilliant, isn't it?"

"Oh."

Betram spun around again. "Don't worry," said Betramos, patting her head. "It's only one night, and as soon as it's over we'll be on our way to the Imperial Capital, and finally out of this barbarian wasteland."

That night, when Deica was locked in her room with a Twin guard outside her door, she prayed to the Makers. Everything that Betram was promising her—travel, excitement, the chance to meet the Emperor—sounded wonderful, but somehow she was getting there all wrong. She felt like she was in jail, the way the Twins told her where to go and what to do. And she couldn't ignore how Betram put down centaurs. Maybe it didn't make sense, but she saw them as her family and her people, and she wanted to stick up for them.

On impulse, she got up and made an archery stance. Slowly, her body settled into the familiar form, and her confusion faded. The words of her grandfather came back to her. *Life always traces the same arc: ready, draw, release.* And then she knew: she had to escape. She was drawn to the breaking point. When the right time came, she would slip away like the arrow slips from the bow, like snow falling from a leaf.

The next morning Betram took her to the Ambassador's estate. It was a beautiful mansion, with stone archways, bronze sculptures, and huge tapestries hanging on the walls, but it failed to make much of an impression on Deica. Finally she entered the Ambassador's office. The Ambassador was a tall, thin Twin, quite old, with a mild demeanor and a distracted look.

"Yes, yes, what have we here, what have we here?" he said, looking back and forth between Deica and Betram. Betram introduced her and began telling the story of their journey from Kerigos to Chiron, starting with a dramatic account of how he single-handedly fought off a rioting mob of centaurs and an angry unicorn to save Deica from certain death.

The Ambassador waved Betram off. "Yes, yes, very good work, I'm sure. Now Deicos, the banquet this evening is a masquerade, a costume ball, if you will. I'm thinking that we will dress you as a satyr. To everyone else, it will seem as though you're an ordinary satyr with no costume. We'll build up their curiosity, showing you around to all the important people but without divulging anything. They're bound to wonder who you are and why you're not wearing a costume. Then, when the time is right, we strip off your disguise, and presto! You are a Single, a Maker, the sensation of the evening, the star of the show. How would you like that?"

"What I'd really like," she said, "is to go out riding, and then practice archery for awhile."

The Ambassador looked momentarily nonplussed, but he quickly spun to show her his other half—an old woman, shorter and plumper than the Ambassador, with a round face and caring eyes. "Oh, my dear boy," she said. "Tell me about riding and archery. Is that what you like?"

"Yes," said Deica. "I'm a very good archer. My grandfather taught me."

"Isn't that nice," she said. "Well, I'm sure you'll have plenty of time for those sorts of things when the banquet is over. But for now, there are a few things that they'll want you to do to prepare for tonight. So why don't you run along with Betram and let him set you up, all right?"

Before Deica had a chance to reply, the Ambassador spun again. "Very good, very good," said the Ambassador's male half, waving her and Betram off. "Well, I'm sure that this will be a grand old time. Looking forward to it, Deicos my boy," he said as he turned away and started reading some papers on his desk.

Deica spent the rest of the day preparing for the banquet. She went from one Twin to another getting dressed and disguised, with Betram and the guards always with her. She was nearly discovered as a girl, but she managed to keep her secret by insisting on some privacy for her underclothes. On top of those, they put on a formal dress tunic, clipped goat's horns to her head, and gave her a false beard and special shoes with goat's hooves on the bottom. The shoes took some getting used to, but she had to admit that it was a good disguise; no one who passed her on the street would think her anything but a teenaged satyr boy.

The day rushed past and the banquet began. It was held in a huge hall, with a forty-foot ceiling, columns of marble pillars lining the room, and long tables piled high with lobster, snake meat, peppered eagle's eggs, and other delicacies. Hundreds of Twins and centaurs were there from the highest ranks of society, dressed in costumes frightening and playful, monstrous and surreal. In one corner, a herd of centaurs dressed as a school of fish cut through the crowd. In another, a Twin spun wildly, one half dressed as a hanged man and the other as his executioner. In front of her a tall Twin with a dragon's head mask stared at her, his big eyes bulging.

She'd been hoping that the party might give her a chance to slip away, but as the evening wore on she grew more and more discouraged. Her Twin guard was always watching her; there seemed to be no hope of escape. She was passed from one Twin to another, quickly presented to centaurs, and just as quickly whisked away. Someone handed her a glass of wine, and she drank. She felt sick, dreading the moment when they would strip away her disguise and everyone would look at her.

Suddenly she felt a cool hand on her wrist, and a voice said, "Hey." She turned to see a Twin only a few years older than she, dressed as a pirate with rough clothes and a sword at his side. His face was handsome with dark hair, and his bright eyes seemed to be laughing at her. "You don't look like you're having fun," he said with a smile.

Deica just smiled weakly, not knowing what to say.

The young Twin turned around to show her his other half—a beautiful young woman, dressed as a princess in an elegant white gown. Her long blonde hair fell in waves down her shoulders. She raised her hand to Deica, palm down. "I'm Corona," she said, smiling. "Pleased to meet you."

Deica wondered if she was supposed to kiss her hand. She put it to her lips and then let it go. Corona looked at her coyly and gave a little laugh. "Deicos," Deica said, awkwardly.

Corona turned around, and the dark young man with laughing eyes was facing her again. "I'm Coronus," he said, shaking her hand. He leaned in close. "Do you want to get out of here?"

Deica looked back at her Twin guard, who was watching her with one half while the other was keeping up an animated conversation with a group of centaurs. "What do you mean?" she asked.

Coronus shrugged. "I hate these parties," he said. "But my father makes me go because he's the Imperial Legate. Let's sneak out, have a few beers, check out the city." He looked at the guard behind her. "I'm sure we could give him the slip. It'd be a good joke on all of them. What do you say?"

This could be her chance. "All right," Deica said. "How do we do it?"

Coronus grinned from ear to ear and leaned in till his face was almost touching hers. He reminded her rather uncomfortably of a

wolf. "Wait fifteen minutes," he said. "Then tell them you have to go to the toilet." He suddenly moved back and turned around, showing her his other half, Corona. She smiled and blew Deica a kiss, then both of them were lost in the crowd.

Fifteen minutes. How long was fifteen minutes? There was no hourglass or sundial in the banquet hall, or one of the elaborate "clocks" that Betram had told her the Zigots made. She did her best to estimate the time, as she was introduced to another round of centaur nobility. Finally she said to her guard, "I don't feel well. I have to use the toilet."

The guard nodded with both heads and took her down a short hallway to a small private toilet with no windows. She entered and the guard stood outside.

Deica waited for a while, wondering what to do next. Then she heard low voices outside. She couldn't make out the words, but one of the voices was female.

After a few minutes, she heard a sudden, cut-off cry and a low thump. A few seconds later Coronus opened the door. "Help me drag him in here," he said evenly, motioning to her guard, now lying unconscious in the hallway.

She stared at Coronus and then at the guard. The guard was a lot bigger than Coronus and a double male. "How'd you do that?" she asked.

"He, ah, had too much to drink," said Coronus. Corona winked at Deica as though sharing a secret joke, but whatever it was, Deica didn't get it. "Help me drag him in here," repeated Coronus, louder.

Deica clumsily grabbed the guard's four boots and helped drag him into the toilet room. Coronus lifted his torsos; together they managed to squeeze him in and shut the door. Then Corona grabbed Deica's wrist with a surprisingly strong grip and pulled her along, as Coronus moved quickly down the hall, saying, "Follow me," over his shoulder, as though she had a choice.

—— Chapter Five ——

WILD HORSES

Coron raced out of the mansion, pulling Deica behind him. They crossed the gardens and passed through a side gate out to a well lit street, busy with centaurs. Waiting for them was a horse-drawn coach led by a burly centaur with a dark beard. He looked away as Coron and Deica arrived.

Coronus opened the coach door with a flourish. "After you, my dear," Corona said with a smile.

Deica peered into the rich, dark interior. It reminded her uncomfortably of Betram's coach. "No, thanks," she said.

Corona laughed. "Come on, Deicos, get inside."

"No, I don't want to go in," Deica said. "How about I ride one of the horses?" Deica felt sure she could handle one of the black steeds drawing the coach, and she was aching to ride.

A look of fury suddenly crossed Corona's face, and she shot a glance at the centaur. He turned to Deica with a cold, measuring stare, like he was judging how easy it would be to break her in half. *What was going on?* Deica glanced nervously up and down the street.

Then Coron spun, and Coronus burst out laughing. "Oh, look at you, Corona," he said. "All bent out of shape just because Deicos doesn't want to play footsie with you. Be a little more subtle, girl. Try playing hard to get. And Digrus—don't be such a horse's ass. You're scaring my new friend.

"Don't worry," Coronus said to Deica. "If you'd rather ride on a saddle than sit in a coach, that's all right with us. In fact, you and Digrus should get along. He's got a rough streak, too." He tipped his pirate cap to the centaur. "He works for my father. He's my bodyguard, so I can't play hooky without him."

Digrus gave Deica a half-smile, and unhooked one of the horses. "We'll ride too," said Coronus. Digrus unhooked another horse for Coron.

Deica climbed into the saddle, still a little wary. "I need to go to my inn," she said. "I'm not coming back here, and I'll need my horse."

Coronus raised an eyebrow, and Deica again had the feeling that he was laughing at her. "Whatever you say, Deicos. Whatever you say."

So Deica and Coron rode quickly through the wide city streets to the inn where she and Betram were staying. First they fetched her bow and arrows from her room, then Deica took Alethra from the stables. Deica felt a rush of joy as she swung herself onto Alethra's back and rode out into the street. It had been too long.

As they left the inn, Coron pulled his horse up and Corona said softly, "Deicos, it's none of my business what you're running away from. But if you want, I know a place where you can rest and plan your next move. What do you say?"

Deica hesitated, still not knowing what to make of Coron. But she didn't have anywhere else to go. She nodded and said, "All right."

Corona smiled and rode ahead. Alethra followed her lead, and Digrus took up the rear, still leading the empty coach.

Coron led her to an estate on the outskirts of the city. It was a sprawling stone mansion, well kept up and with many rooms, but all the windows were shuttered. They passed a gatehouse and a guard waved them through. Coronus gave their horses and baggage to the stable-girl and steered Deica to a side door.

The door led into a small, dimly lit room with a long bar. Behind the bar was a middle-aged female centaur with a worn face and long dark hair. She was dressed a low-cut red gown with a golden necklace and earrings. A cloud of perfume surrounded her.

"Good to see you, Coron," said the woman. Her mouth smiled, but her eyes were dull.

Digrus stood by the door while Coronus led Deica to the bar. He leaned back and his face broke into a broad grin. "It's been quite a trip," Coronus said with a laugh. "But we finally made it. We're safe here."

"Where's here?" Deica asked, looking around. The walls were covered with tapestries and paintings depicting centaurs, satyrs, and other creatures—most of them naked, some having sex. They were so many and so vivid that the room felt crowded.

"Medena's House of Delights," laughed the centaur woman. "I'm Medena." Her tone was cheerful, but something about it seemed forced. Deica took her limp hand uncertainly, and quickly let it go.

Coronus laughed. "Don't worry," he said. "I didn't bring you here to sample Medena's delights, though you're welcome to whatever you can afford. But I figured that no one at the Ambassador's masquerade would look for you here. You can plan your next move in peace."

But the room didn't feel very peaceful to Deica. She looked up, trying to avoid the graphic portraits assaulting her eyes. On the ceiling was a painting of a...Single? Someone with two legs and two arms, like her. But it was a man—a heavyset man, white-skinned and naked, his eyes wide and his mouth open in a crazed grin. His huge hands grasped the haunches of a black mare, her face frozen in terror as he took her from behind. Deica stared, then looked away.

Coronus glanced upwards and yawned. "Birth of a nation, huh?"

"What?"

He looked at Deica quizzically. "Aeneas creating the first centaur," he said. "Though most paintings don't show him having quite so much fun."

Something—anger?—flickered briefly behind Medena's eyes, but was quickly replaced by her usual vacant stare. She broke in loudly, saying to Deica:

"You want me to set you up? You like nymphs? You like centaurs? We've got the best in the city."

From the ceiling came the sound of hoof beats and male cheering. Deica's head jerked up in fear; the painting was so real that for a second she thought that the figures were coming alive. But then she realized that the sounds were coming from the room above.

Medena didn't look up. "Hope the boys don't bother you," she said. "They've got a couple of mares up there, and things can get pretty wild."

Mixed in with the cheering was the sound of horses whinnying in terror. "Horses?" Deica asked. "They're centaurs, and they've got horses?"

"They get whatever they want, as long as they pay for it. Horses are real popular around mating season."

The cheering grew louder, drowning out the screams of the horses, and the hoof beats stomped in rhythm. Deica shuddered.

"I think horses are not quite up my friend's alley," said Coronus. "Let's start with a pitcher of beer."

Medena drew a pitcher while Corona turned and spoke to Deica. "This place is a little rough for you, isn't it?" she asked, gently putting her hand on Deica's arm.

It reminds me of a tomb, Deica wanted to say, but somehow she didn't think that Corona would understand.

"You're not like most satyrs, Deicos," said Corona.

Deica had almost forgotten her disguise. She didn't know how it could have slipped her mind: she was sweating like a pig under the false beard and her feet ached from walking on the goat-foot stilts. But at least the disguise still seemed intact.

Coronus poured a beer for Deica and one for himself. He raised his glass.

"Let's drink to your freedom, Deicos," he said. "What's next for you?"

Good question. She had no money, no friends, and nowhere to go. Maybe Coron was right that Betram and the other Twins wouldn't look for her here, but she didn't like this place and she didn't trust Coron or Medena. What could she do?

And the disguise was killing her. Her face was hot and itchy and she could hardly walk, but more than that she felt sick pretending to be something she wasn't. She hadn't told the truth since she left home, not even to Gustus. She was tired of lying. She decided to come clean.

"What's next for me is to tell the truth," she said. "I'm not what you think I am."

Then she took off her satyr disguise—first the false beard and bushy eyebrows, then the goat horns clipped to her hair, and finally the wooden stilts made to look like goat hooves. Coronus and Medena stared at her, amazed, as she peeled away each layer.

"I was never a satyr," Deica began. "I was born to a centaur family..." And, in between big gulps of her beer, she told them the story of her life, from her childhood in Delos to her life with Gustus and her travels with Betram, ending at the Ambassador's Masquerade.

Coronus and Medena listened carefully. Coronus seemed to have something in mind; he interrupted several times to ask about her race and whether there were others like her: "Did you ever hear of others like you?", "Did Betram mention that there were others?" And when she told him each time that she'd never heard of anyone else, he seemed annoyed. Medena asked no questions, but as Deica told her story a strange look crossed her face: fascination, perhaps, or fear.

Finally she finished, having saved her final secret for last. "And one more thing: my name isn't Deicos. It's Deica. I learned to shoot like a boy, but I'm not a boy. I'm a girl."

Medena and Coronus reacted strangely to this news. Medena looked suddenly pained and gave a little cry, like something had died inside her. Coronus stared at Deica, and then burst out laughing.

"You're a girl!" he cried. "Well, no wonder Corona couldn't get anywhere with you! I was beginning to think she'd lost her touch. Ha ha, a girl! Ha ha!"

Deica waited for him to settle down, but he just kept laughing. "Well, that would have been good to know! What do you think of that, Medena? She's a girl!" Medena said nothing.

He turned to Digrus. "How about you, Digrus? Come and have a beer with us. I hear you're hard up this season. Maybe you'll get lucky with Deica." Coronus burst out laughing again.

Deica started to tell him angrily that that wasn't funny, but for some reason her jaw was slow to move, and all that came out was an unintelligible, "Thaaas—"

Coronus ignored her, and wiped tears from his eyes. "Well, the Twin Senate wouldn't have been too happy to find that out. You wouldn't have made a very effective puppet King without a scepter." He giggled.

Puppet King? What was he talking about? Deica looked sharply at him. Or, rather, she tried to look sharply. Her neck was stiff, and felt like it was turning in quicksand.

Digrus walked over. He wasn't laughing. Nervous, Deica tried to rise, but her legs wouldn't hold her weight, and she fell off her chair, dropping her beer mug. It shattered on the stone floor.

"Oh, what's wrong?" asked Coronus. He bent down and helped her up. "Too much to drink?"

She hadn't had much—only a glass of wine at the Masquerade and a glass of beer here. And she could still think clearly. But her body didn't seem to be moving right. She tried to say, "My legs won't move," but it came out, "Mmlss wannoo."

Coronus held her up and turned her to face Digrus. "You know, Digrus," he said. "If I didn't know better, I'd say that someone had drugged Deica's beer. What do you think, Digrus? Did you drug Deica's beer?"

Digrus cracked his knuckles and scowled. He said nothing.

"No, no," said Coronus. "You're not that subtle, and besides, you were on the other side of the room." Coronus turned Deica around to face Medena across the bar, holding her like a rag doll, her arms flopping uselessly by her sides. She could see and hear everything, but her muscles were completely unresponsive.

"How about you, Medena? Did you drug Deica's beer?" Medena's face was a mask. She said nothing.

"No," said Coronus. "I didn't think so. Well, if you didn't do it, and Digrus didn't do it, who could it have been? Who drugged Deica's beer?" He looked from Medena to Digrus. Medena looked down. Digrus cracked his knuckles.

The voice of Corona came from behind him. "It was you, pretty boy."

"Ah, my ace student, my star pupil, 10 out of 10 again!" cried Coronus. "Not that you had much competition from these two dunces." Coronus turned Deica to face him. "Not to worry, my dear," he said. "A little Blackwort won't hurt you, just make you easier to travel with. You see, we're going to take a trip out into the wilderness, under the open stars, where no one can hear you scream. Would you like that?"

Coronus grabbed Deica's hair and pulled her lolling head up and down. "Oh, you would!" he exclaimed. "That means so much to me."

He leaned in close and drew his tongue slowly along his teeth. "It's a good thing you're in a storytelling mood, my dear, because before the night is over you're going to tell me everything. I think you held back just now, but I'll bet you'll answer my questions a little more completely when I'm peeling the flesh from your bones."

Coronus threw Deica roughly into Digrus' arms. "I'll be back soon with transportation," he said. "In the meantime, Digrus and Medena will keep you comfortable." He turned, and Corona touched Deica's hand sympathetically. "Look on the bright side, Deica. There are worse things than being flayed alive. You could have ended up an ugly old whore like Medena." Medena flinched, and Corona laughed and laughed as she and Coronus sauntered out the door.

Digrus swung Deica over his shoulder and carried her through a narrow hallway behind the bar and into a small bedroom. He threw her on the floor and tied and gagged her—not that she could speak or move anyway. Medena left and closed the door. Digrus stayed. He looked out of place, such a large centaur in a small room.

After a few minutes Deica began hearing load moans of pleasure from the room next door. Digrus shifted uncomfortably. The sounds became louder, especially the calls of what sounded like more than one female centaur. Digrus paced back and forth, and glared at Deica as though she were somehow to blame.

A few minutes later, Medena came in again. She said sympathetically, "Digrus, why don't you go next door and give one of the girls a toss? It's on the house."

Digrus hesitated, looking at Deica. Medena added, "Don't worry. You can be back in time. I won't tell Coron." He quickly nodded and then nearly galloped out of the room.

Medena closed the door. Her face seemed to crack open and she burst into tears. She threw herself at Deica's side crying, "Forgive me. Please forgive me." It was like a dam had broken inside of her.

Gagged and paralyzed, all Deica could do was grunt. When she did, Medena pulled herself together. "Yes," she said, "of course." Quickly she scooped Deica up and put her on her back, then trotted out of the room, down the hall, and out the door. She took Deica to a small stable in the back of a guardhouse. Alethra was there and whinnied to see her. But Medena ignored her and walked through the stalls and into a back room filled with hay.

She gently put Deica down and cut her bonds and gag. "They won't look here," Medena said. "But just in case, I'll put you under the hay."

Medena held up a small traveling bag. "There's some food and some money in here. I'll be back by dawn to let you know if it's safe. But if I'm not back don't wait for me. Take your horse and ride away."

She looked into Deica's eyes. "Ride far away, Deica. Coron and Digrus are with the Imperial Secret Service. The Emperor wants you dead, you and all your kind. They'll come after you. They won't rest and they won't have mercy."

Deica managed to say, "W-why?"

"I think he's afraid that one of you will claim his throne. Maybe he wouldn't be if he knew you're a girl, but don't take that chance."

That wasn't what she was asking. She shook her head, repeating, "Why?" and looked at the bag at her side.

Then Medena understood. She sighed quietly. "When I was a little girl my mother used to tell me about the Makers, how they were kind and good and always watching over us," she said. "But she didn't believe it. She told me it was a lie the first time she—" Medena's face tightened in pain, "—when she brought me here. She sold me that night for six pieces of silver. She said she was showing me the truth about life."

Medena's tears began to flow again. "That night I learned—I thought I learned—what life was really about. And so I stayed here, and became that. I didn't forget the stories. I told them to—to a child I know. But I didn't believe them. I thought it was just pretty lies. Now, to find out that it's all true—that you're real..." Medena's voice trembled.

She brushed Deica's hair—gently, as though she were afraid to touch her. "If I'd met you earlier, things might have been different for me. It's too late for that, but if I can save the life of a Maker, maybe my own life isn't such a waste after all."

"Good-bye, Deica," she said, and kissed her forehead. Then she carefully buried Deica and the bag under the straw, deep enough that no one would see her but shallow enough that she could breathe. With a final squeeze of her hand, Medena left.

Deica didn't know how many hours she spent under the straw. She heard noises—the clomps and snorts of the horses in the next room, hoof beats of centaurs in the street, faint cries of cheering from the house—until finally she fell asleep.

She woke to the sound of the stable door thrown open, and the clatter of hoof beats in the next room. There were whispered voices, too low to hear, and the sound of latches turning and horses being roused from sleep, as though someone was searching each stall. Nervously, Deica tried to move. She couldn't even wiggle a finger.

Suddenly, from the main house came the loud clanging of bells—the sound of an alarm. She heard low swearing, and then whoever was in the stable ran outside. For a long time afterwards Deica heard the movement of horses and the muffled voices of centaurs outside, but no one came into the stable again, and in the end she fell asleep.

When she woke again the warm morning light was shining through the windows. It was past dawn, and Medena wasn't back. Deica cleared her throat and wiggled her arms and legs. Still stiff, but now she could ride.

She got up, brushed the straw from her clothes, and stretched. Then she heard a door open in the next room. She crouched and peered through the boards of the wooden door separating her from the horses. A young centaur girl, twelve or thirteen, with tangled dark hair and hands and hooves rough from work, walked among the horses, saddling and bridling them. Her face was red as though she'd been crying. She spoke to the horses gently as she made them ready to leave.

Deica watched nervously as the girl took Alethra out of her stall and saddled her, strapping on her baggage, including Deica's bow and quiver of arrows. Deica didn't want to show herself, but who knew where the girl was going, or when she'd be back?

Standing straight up, Deica swung the door open, strode forward, and announced, "That's my horse. I'll take her."

The centaur girl jumped and stared at her. "Who are you?"

"I'm...I'm the owner of that horse. And I was just about to take her for a ride."

The girl kept starting at Deica, and said, "If you try to hurt me, I'm going to call the guards—" She looked behind her and started backing out the door.

"No, no, wait! Please don't call the guards. I won't hurt you. I just—" Deica's arms fell to her sides. "What's your name?" she asked.

"Synthe. What's yours?"

"Deica. Synthe, this is my horse, but—it's kind of a secret. Medena said that I could stay here, but not to let anyone know."

The girl's eyes grew wide. "Medena said you could stay here?"

"Yes. What is it? What's wrong?"

"Medena's dead. They found her beaten to death last night. Didn't you hear the alarm?"

A wave of emotion hit Deica. *They were looking for me. She could have given me up and saved herself, but she didn't.* Deica stumbled backwards and sat down on the floor.

The centaur girl approached uncertainly. "Are you all right?"

Deica's head was swimming with a thousand wild thoughts. But the familiar taste of fear overrode them all. She had to get out of here. If she left now, she could get out of the city before they found her.

Deica forced herself up, said, "Yes. But I have to leave," and put her foot in Alethra's stirrups, starting to mount.

"You're a Maker, aren't you?" asked Synthe.

Deica stopped. "I—Why do you ask that?"

"You look like a Maker. When I was young, Medena used to tell me about the Makers, how they live way up on Earth where everyone is happy, and they're always kind to each other. But when I got older she didn't want to talk about them anymore."

Deica put her foot back on the ground. "Synthe, was Medena your mother?"

Synthe shook her head. "I don't have a mother. But Medena let me stay here. She taught me to take care of the horses. She was nice to me, just like she said the Makers were."

"I'm sorry that she's gone, Synthe," said Deica. "She was—She was nice to me, too."

"So are you a Maker?" asked Synthe again.

"I—I guess I look like one, so people think I am. Some of them want to kill me for it. But that was why Medena saved my life. I—My parents were centaurs."

"But what are you?"

What am I? The memory of her childhood's darkest night rose up again, but this time she didn't run away from it. Medena had walked bravely into death for Deica; the least that Deica could do was face an eight year old truth. "I always thought of myself as a centaur," said Deica, "until one night when I was nine…" She paused at the edge, then plunged ahead, "I went into the forest."

"The forest, where I grew up, wasn't just trees—it was the Wild Lands, where evil lived. We were never supposed to go there. But I heard a song, a beautiful song, and I followed it. There were people, singing and dancing around a fire. Six of them—old crones, witches, but they looked like me, with two legs and two arms, fingers and toes like mine. They had a pot with some kind of stew in it, smoking and giving off a strange smell, green and earthy.

"I tried to hide, but they saw me and pulled me out of the bushes. They held me in front of the fire and started poking me and asking me questions, like what took me so long to come out, what the centaurs thought of me, whether I could see the future or do magic. They acted like they knew me—they called themselves my 'aunts' and called me 'sister-daughter.' I didn't understand, and I was too terrified to say anything. I thought they were going to eat me.

"But they just laughed, and after a while they seemed to get tired of me and went back to singing and dancing and eating their stew. And then the last thing they did before they left, they—they *changed.*

"Their skin became scaly, their fingers turned into claws, their teeth sharpened, necks lengthened, they sprouted wings and grew bigger than a house—huge monstrous winged Serpents. They must have been the oldest Children of the Serpent, Elder Worms we call them. And they cackled and took off into the sky, saying they'd see me again someday.

"I ran back home, and to this day I've never told anyone this: not my grandfather, not my grandmother, no one. I thought it meant that I was really one of them, that I was a Serpent in disguise, maybe that I'd been switched at birth. And I was sure that if anyone knew, they would kill me. Later, an Elder Worm attacked one of the villages nearby. I don't know if it was one of the ones I saw, but I was so terrified I could barely think. I don't know what I was more afraid of:

that it would kill me or that it would tell them that I was really a Serpent. I just wanted to get as far away as I could.

"But now I come here, and everyone says I look like a Maker, and that just makes me more confused. Are the Makers Serpents? Are the Serpents Makers? What am I? I don't know, Synthe. But whatever the truth is I want to know. I've come a long way from home because I've been afraid of finding out, but I think the answer's back in the Wild Lands, so that's where I'm going next."

Deica couldn't tell how much Synthe had understood, but Synthe nodded. "I'm leaving too," she said. "Medena didn't like having the horses here. She said that if anything ever happened to her I should take the horses and go to Milo the farmer. He's got a farm a few miles outside the city. She set it all up, that he would take me on as a farmhand if I brought the horses."

"I'll come with you," Deica said. "At least part way. Will the guards let us past?"

"They might," said Synthe. "But I think there's someone watching the main entrance. I saw a strange coach across the street."

"Then how do we get out?"

"There's a gap in the back fence. We can lead the horses out, and there are trails that run to Milo's farm."

Deica nodded, and the two of them finished gathering the horses, twelve young mares, and led them out into the backyard, through the gap in the fence, and into the woods behind the estate. Deica rode Alethra and followed Synthe as Synthe led the other horses. The forest trail was quiet and beautiful; it reminded Deica of home.

When they reached the final turn, Synthe said, "This goes to Milo's farm."

"All right. Good luck, Synthe. I'd take you there myself, but it's safer for you if I don't."

"Which way are you going?"

"Outwards. I'll ride the Milk Roads, and use the Inward star as a guide. One way or another, I'll reach the Wild Lands."

"Can I touch you before you go? I've never touched a Maker before."

Deica nodded. Synthe reached her hand up and gently touched Deica's arm, petting her gingerly, with a look of intense concentration.

Deica bent and kissed Synthe's forehead. "May the Makers bless you, Synthe," she said. Synthe's eyes grew wide and a big smile spread across her face.

Deica smiled back, then wheeled Alethra around and galloped down the trail, her hands on Alethra's mane, her hair and tunic flying loose, riding for the Wild Lands like an arrow shot into the sky.

The story of the Wheel continues at www.cityofif.com...

—— ACKNOWLEDGEMENTS ——

I'd like to thank everyone who helped me create this book: my wife Mïa, who's not only the love of my life and my guardian angel but also the source of my inspiration; everyone who reviewed the manuscript, especially my parents, my sister Martha, and my friend Dick Hill, all of whom gave me valuable feedback that improved the book; Patrick McEvoy and Leigh Dragoon, whose illustrations were both beautiful and faithful to the text and who were a joy to work with throughout; Lee Moyer, whose book design brought out the best in the illustrations; Morris Rosenthal and Aaron Shepard, whose books on publishing and typography were tremendously helpful; and, of course, everyone who played the original storygame and who's helped build the City of IF since then. There's not enough space to mention everyone on the site, but I especially want to thank the "City Council:" Mordok, Smee, Reiso, Ravenwing, Random, D-Lotus, and saxon215. I couldn't have done this without you.

Printed in the United States
29381LVS00002B/1-81